for AM [handwritten inscription]

The

Adventures

Of

SuperBaby

Book 1: The first nine months

from Ed Wicke [handwritten signature]

by Ed Wicke

Super

8 In the Beginning...

SuperBaby's parents don't know that he can read, or that his best friends are a rat, a mouse, a cat, a brick and an empty cereal box. They don't even know he can fly.

22 Friends

Your parents will probably choose the wrong friends for you, so it's better to find your own. But don't let your friends eat one another.

37 Enemies

Surely everyone loves babies? Oops... Maybe not the scary people who live across the road!

71 Babysitters

Your parents don't know what the babysitter gets up to after they walk out the door.

Baby

90 The Mystery of Grandma's Knickers

Thievery, trickery, hair dye, and the first case for a Baby Detective. And introducing Connie the Crow: the greatest con artist in the neighbourhood.

127 Baby Steps and Baby Love

Ah... Holiday romance!

143 Supermarket Adventures

Always remember that strangers are BAD...

170 The Tale of "Bad the Burglar"

... And burglars can't be trusted, either. Even when they become investment bankers.

189 Babynapped

Being kidnapped at Christmas isn't fun... unless you're SuperBaby!

For Angela, my Angel.

Some other books by Ed Wicke:

Ed Wicke

The Adventures of

SuperBaby

Published by BlacknBlue Press UK
13 Dellands, Overton, Hampshire, England
blacknbluepress@hotmail.com

This book copyright © September 2016 Ed Wicke
Cover copyright © September 2016 Janine van Moosel
Illustrations copyright © September 2016 Janine van Moosel

Additional illustrations by:
David (who caused the first SuperBaby story to be told)
Ara
Zoe and Ben
Asher, Sienna and Heidi
Jonah
Holly
Rachel Eggington
Ed Wicke
Angela Wicke

ISBN 978-0-9930460-4-9

The Voices

SuperBaby sounds like a cute and friendly baby. He knows his parents wouldn't be able to cope with his super-powered language skills, so he babbles to them in baby talk instead. Like all babies, he gets excited very quickly and sad very quickly. He'll fall asleep half way through a conversation, or wake up at three in the morning to eat some chocolate spread and read his cereal box.

SuperBaby's family talk to him in the over-bright, over-simple way that adoring adults use with babies. **The Father** sounds friendly, and sometimes puzzled (maybe that's because he's about always getting blamed for things SuperBaby does). **The Mother** sounds fussy and rather tired and very loving. **Grandma** sounds kind. She also sounds like she thinks she knows best.

Cat the Cat is a relaxed, friendly cat who spends a lot of time sleeping. She has a high, sweet, mewing voice and makes cute *Prrrrrp!* sounds at SuperBaby's window when she wants to come in. She's calm and sensible and loyal. She doesn't understand why SuperBaby wouldn't eat the mouse she brought him, but now that Mick is the baby's friend, she'll protect that mouse with her life.

Mick the Mouse's squeakings always sound rather scared, because being a mouse *is* scary - what with owls and cats and foxes and mousetraps and burglars who might steal your whiskers.

Rocky the Rat - well, he's a bit rough and ready, right? If you want some second hand greasy chips, pickled onions or water pistols, Rocky's your man. Or rat.

Connie the Crow is cheeky, cheerful and chirpy. She's a fast-talking con artist who will tie you up in verbal knots... and while you're trying to untie yourself, she'll have nicked all your clothes pegs, put them in an envelope and posted them to China.

Bad the Burglar sounds like a posh burglar - or a rough banker - or a burglar banker pretending to be Santa. He always sounds annoyed. He always sounds like he wants something, probably your money. After the incident involving SuperBaby and the mysteriously silent **Rick the Brick**, Bad the B sounds worried as well.

Mad Mary is that nightmare person you'll learn to avoid by crossing the street, climbing a tree or jumping off a cliff. If you start a conversation with her about anything *(Hi! Do you like kittens?)*, she'll turn it into an argument and then shout at you at high speed for hours and call you names if you don't give in and say she's right.

Lady Beatrice is posh. **Sir Bertie** isn't. She has a lovely, slow, annoyingly superior voice. He talks quickly and doesn't waste time pronouncin' the beginnin' or end of a word unless 'e absolutely 'as to. She sounds totally certain about everything. He sounds totally bothered and confused about it all.

Grump the Politician sounds like he totally loves himself and the sound of his own voice. **Maria** thinks she's adorable and thinks you should think so too. **Thug** sounds like he wants to punch you.

Ben the Box says nothing at all. Because he's a box.

In the Beginning...

At half past midnight on the first day of April, SuperBaby was born.

He didn't like it out here in the cold, dry air. He didn't like the smell of the hospital room and he *hated* the bright lights that hurt his eyes. He'd loved being inside his mother, where everything was soft and warm and dark. He had felt safe and happy there, with soothing water all around him and his mother's voice murmuring in the background.

'I'm not having this,' he said to himself. 'I'm going to hold my breath, and they'll have to put me back inside!'

So he squeezed his eyes shut and held his breath.

The nurse who had just delivered him gave him a little push and a poke, to get him to breathe.

'Come on, baby: Breathe!' she urged.

'UnnUnn!' he grunted, shaking his head.

The nurse gave him a little jiggle up and down. '*Please* breathe!' she whispered.

'UnnUnnUnnUnn**Unn**!' he insisted, shaking his head even more and clamping his lips tight.

The nurse was worried now, and gave him a tiny slap on his tiny botty.

'Ow! Waaaaaaaaaaaaaaa!'

While he was having a good (and very loud) cry, he looked around at all the new things. He'd never seen a bed before, or all this hospital equipment with wires and glowing lights. He hadn't even seen a wall before. He thought, *Actually, this looks really interesting. Maybe I'll stay a while!*

But he wasn't happy about being smacked on the botty, even though it was a very tiny smack for a good reason. And because he was a baby, he didn't know it was wrong to take revenge or hit back. He didn't know that this just makes things worse! So he waited until the nurse had her back turned, and he reached across with his little hand and –

Whack! He gave *her* a slap on the botty, too!

'Ohhhh!' she exclaimed, covering her backside with her hands and looking around to see who had slapped her in such a personal place.

There were only four people in the room: the nurse, the mother (who was lying on the bed), SuperBaby and SuperBaby's father. The nurse pointed a finger at...

SuperBaby's father.

She said sternly, '*You* slapped me right on the -' and she pointed at the place of the slap.

'It wasn't me!' said SuperBaby's father. 'I didn't touch you! I promise!'

The nurse wagged her finger at him and said, 'Well, it wasn't the baby, was it?'

So SuperBaby's father got blamed for something SuperBaby had done. And not for the last time!

SuperBaby opened his mouth to say, *'It wasn't him,*

it was me!' But he stopped himself. Maybe it would be better not to tell anyone about his super powers. He didn't want to scare them. And it was going to be such fun pretending to be an ordinary baby!

'Gah gah goo goo!' he laughed out loud.

Cat the Cat and Mick the Mouse

When you're a baby, certain things happen to you for the first time. For instance, SuperBaby made his first friend.

His first friend was their cat, who was very good at putting holes in curtains, trousers and any small creatures she caught in the garden. SuperBaby didn't understand about names yet, so he just called her Cat the Cat (though not when anyone was listening).

One morning, Cat the Cat appeared on the window ledge outside SuperBaby's window and scratched at the glass, calling out: '*Prrrrppppp!*' – which means 'Let me in!'

SuperBaby checked to make sure that no one was around. Then he flew to the window, opened it and flew back to his cot. The cat came in, carrying something in her mouth.

She jumped onto the railing of SuperBaby's cot and dropped something grey and furry at SuperBaby's feet.

'*Meowwww.* I've got a present for you,' said Cat the Cat proudly. 'I thought you must be tired of drinking milk all the time. Get your teeth into that!'

'I haven't got any teeth yet,' said SuperBaby. 'What's that furry thing?' He pointed at it.

'It's a mouse,' said Cat the Cat. 'And they're really tasty! If you don't want it, I'll eat it.'

SuperBaby looked at the tiny grey mouse. It opened its eyes and gave a sad little squeak.

SuperBaby picked up the mouse and said, 'Awww. You're so cute! You can be my new friend. I know about names now, so I'll call you Mick the Mouse!'

The Cat was horrified. 'No!' she exclaimed. 'Mice are food. You *eat* them! They're full of vitamins!'

SuperBaby pointed at Mick the Mouse. 'But he's my friend now. Are you allowed to eat your friends?' (He was a baby, so he didn't know the rules).

Cat the Cat said, 'No, you don't eat your friends. You help them when they need you, and you play with them. Waste of a good snack, though....'

So the three friends had a few happy games until they felt tired. Mick the Mouse was tired first, because he'd had an exciting morning. He had been chased – caught – let go – caught again – carried up a tree – then across to the window ledge – and dropped into a baby's cot. So he curled up next to SuperBaby and fell asleep.

Cat the Cat yawned and curled up on the other side of the baby and dozed off, too.

SuperBaby smiled as he fell asleep, with one arm around Cat the Cat and the other around Mick the Mouse. He had two friends now – life was good!

Meanwhile, his mother had gone out for the first time since bringing the baby back from the hospital.

She'd said to SuperBaby's father:

'I'm just going to the shop to buy a pint of milk. Can you look after the baby while I'm out?'

The father nodded but didn't look up from the book he was reading.

She added, 'You need to listen out for his crying, and go to him immediately.'

'The baby will be fine,' said the father, still reading his book.

'And if he's *too* quiet, you need to go check on him as well. *Immediately.*'

'Okay,' said the father, turning a page.

The mother ran to the corner shop, bought some milk and ran back again. As she stepped in the door, she called to the father: 'Has the baby been all right?'

He looked at his watch. 'You've only been gone three minutes. Of course the baby's all right!'

She put the milk in the fridge, then crept quietly up the stairs, slowly opened the baby's door, peeked inside and …

'*Aaaaaaahh!*' she screamed.

SuperBaby's father came running upstairs. SuperBaby's mother was not happy with him.

'I leave you alone with the baby for ten seconds,' she scolded, 'and look what you've done! You opened his window!'

'Ummm… It wasn't me.'

'Well, it wasn't me, and it certainly wasn't the baby! *You* opened his window, so now his room is the wrong temperature. And look over there – the cat has come inside and jumped into his cot!'

'It wasn't me!'

SuperBaby's mother took a step closer to the cot and looked more carefully… and screamed again.

'Help! A mouse! There's a mouse in the baby's bed!'

Mick the Mouse had been having a lovely dream about flying… and then the dream seemed to come true, because SuperBaby's mother picked up Mick the Mouse and threw him out the window.

'Mmmmmsqueak…zzz…squeak? SQUEAAAʌκ!

Cat the Cat woke up, ran across the room, jumped onto the window ledge and disappeared into the branches of the oak tree outside.

SuperBaby woke to find his mother pointing at

him and shouting, so he started to cry. He cried, was fed, changed, cried, fed, changed, cried, fed, changed … and fell asleep again.

His mother said to his father, 'You are in so much trouble just now!'

SuperBaby's father was in trouble again for something SuperBaby had done. Not for the last time!

About an hour later, Cat the Cat meowed at the window again until SuperBaby woke: so SuperBaby flew across and opened the window.

He sat on the window ledge next to her, kicking his feet and watching the people in the garden across the road, who were chopping things with what looked like giant scissors.

'Did you find Mick the Mouse?' asked SuperBaby.

'Yep,' said the cat. 'I found Mick the Mouse!' She gave the baby a nudge and a big wink – and patted her tummy with one paw.

'You ate my friend!' cried SuperBaby.

'Nah - I was winking. Didn't you see?'

'Ummmm…. What's a wink?' asked SuperBaby.

'This.' The cat winked again. 'That means I'm telling you a joke.'

'What's a joke?' He had never heard one before.

Cat the Cat explained, 'A joke is when you pretend something to make someone else laugh.'

'It didn't make me laugh!' SuperBaby said miserably, and began to cry. 'You ate my friend!'

Cat the Cat said, 'Shhhh! Your parents will hear us! Look: I *didn't* eat Mick the Mouse, because he's our friend. You don't eat your friends, remember? I looked for him all around the neighbourhood, but I couldn't find him.'

SuperBaby cried louder. 'That's even worse!' he sobbed. 'Mick the Mouse is lost forever!'

The people in the garden across the road heard the crying. They looked up at SuperBaby's window and shook their garden tools at him, shouting angrily.

SuperBaby didn't like people shouting at him, so cried even more. Then he fell off the window ledge … did a triple somersault with two full spins… and flew back to his cot.

Because he was a baby, he cried for a long time

about Mick the Mouse until his mother came and picked him up for a comforting cuddle (and chased the cat out of the room again).

SuperBaby had a good morning after that. He was played with and fed and changed and played with and fed and changed and… you get the idea.

That afternoon, his mother carried him to the living room window so he could watch the children coming home from school. He kicked his little legs to show her that he wanted to go running and playing like the big children.

'How sweet!' she said. 'But you'll have to wait another year before you can do that!'

SuperBaby laughed and said, 'No I wo- *Oops... Bee-boo gurgle wurgle!*' He didn't want to frighten her.

Just then a stone came flying through the air and bounced off the window pane, startling SuperBaby and making him cry.

'That's the bad boy from next door!' said his mother. 'He's always throwing stones, which is very naughty: he might hurt someone, or break something! There, there, don't cry…. Nap time, baby!'

SuperBaby had a good nap. When he woke up, he had a rather uncomfortable feeling:

'Uh-oh… Messy nappy!'

He started making the special baby cry that goes something like *'Waaaaaa! MssyNppy!'* when he heard a sound from outside. A sort of *Mrrowwww!* Sound.

'I know that voice!' he said. 'That's Cat the Cat's voice! She's in trouble! I must *save* Cat the Cat!'

So he flew out the window…

Bonk! He rubbed his head. 'Oops! Must open the window first!'

Now he flew out and circled the block of houses. He zigzagged left and right, from one side of the road to the other. He flew over the man and woman in the garden across the road.

Oh no – they looked up and saw him!

The man snapped his garden shears at the baby and the woman shook her fist. Maybe that was just their way of saying hello? So SuperBaby waved back.

He sped away and searched around the houses on his own side of the road. *There she was!*

Poor Cat the Cat was trapped against the fence in a corner of next door's garden. She had found Mick the Mouse and was protecting him from the boy next door, who was pelting them with stones and sticks, shouting 'Got you!' The animals were dodging from side to side, looking frightened.

This was a job for SuperBaby!

He flew over the boy's head and shouted down at him, 'Stop that!'

The boy looked all around, turning in a circle. No one was there. He picked up another stone.

SuperBaby shouted, 'Put that stone down!'

The boy whispered, 'Who said that? Is that a ghost? Is it... *God?* Or... Is it the *devil?*'

But he threw the stone anyway.

SuperBaby said sternly, 'Don't throw stones. It's a bad thing to do!'

'Ha!' said the boy. 'You can't stop me, ghost!' He picked up another stone.

'You'll be sorry!' warned SuperBaby.

The boy thought about this for a long time. Then he said, 'No I won't!' And he threw the stone.

SuperBaby said to himself, 'What can I do? I've got to stop him! He's hurting my friends! But I'm just a baby, I don't have any weapons... oh... I do have *one.*'

He gave a little wiggle…

… and his very messy nappy slipped off his legs…

… and he gave it a kick as it dropped…

… so it turned upside down in the air…

… and landed upside down on the boy's head!

The boy screamed. From inside the nappy came a muffled voice: 'The world's gone dark! And it smells so bad!' Then the boy ran inside with the nappy still on his head.

'I *told* you you'd be sorry!' shouted SuperBaby.

Friends

When you're the first baby, people buy too many presents for you. Your parents then have to write letters to their friends and relations, thanking

them for the fifty-seven toys and woolly hats that are now gathering dust in the attic, sitting on shelves in charity shops or heading for the dustbin.

SuperBaby preferred his real furry friends to the army of cuddly toys that kept invading his room. He was especially suspicious of a big green teddy bear that Grandma had given him.

He loved Grandma, but she was a poor judge of toys. Grandma insisted that the bear was cute and cuddly, and she named it Green Teddy. SuperBaby thought it was scary and called it Evil Teddy.

The morning after Grandma bought the bear, SuperBaby woke to find Evil Teddy lying right next to him, its scary green eyes staring into his own. He screamed and threw the teddy out the window.

After that, he was always trying to get rid of Evil Teddy, but his parents always found it and brought it back. Every time Grandma came, she discovered Evil Teddy in a different place: in the bin in SuperBaby's room… hanging from a branch of the tree outside… stuck on the roof… trapped under the rear car wheel… upside down in the toilet….

His father was always blamed for this, of course!

In a corner of SuperBaby's room was a big cupboard full of fluffy toys he didn't want. His parents rarely looked inside it, so he made a house for Mick the Mouse there. Mick could cuddle in amongst the furry things; and whenever SuperBaby was lonely, he had a friend near at hand.

Ben the Box

Your first taste of baby cereal comes as a wonderful surprise. SuperBaby's mother had bought a small box of it, and showed it to the baby. On its front was a picture of a happy baby, with a bowl +and a spoon. On the back and sides it had a lot of those puzzling squiggly lines that SuperBaby kept seeing in random places at home and on their walks to town.

'Look, baby!' exclaimed his mother. 'Now that you're four months old, you get to try your first baby cereal! Isn't that exciting?'

SuperBaby wasn't sure what he was supposed to do, so he made some of the baby sounds he had been practising that morning.

'Boopee doo floppa?' he asked. 'Ooggee googoo bah?'

'Clever baby!' she said. 'He knows it's something nice!'

And it *was* nice – it was the most wonderful thing he'd ever tasted! He cried when it was all gone, and held out his little hands for the box.

'Look, baby!' she said, pointing at the side of the box. 'See those words? They say it has *sugar* in it, and *rice* and *milk powder!* You like all those!'

SuperBaby stared at the squiggles on the box. So *that's* what all the funny marks on boxes and newspapers and books were! They were *words!* Hooray! Now whenever he was bored in his cot, he could teach himself to read! He began running one tiny finger across the letters.

'Ah, how sweet - he's pretending to read!' said his mother.

'Bah-beebuh doppa doodah!' SuperBaby replied.

And from that day on, he took Ben the Box with him everywhere, reading him again and again. He especially loved the word "sugar".

At night he slept with Ben the Box tucked in next to him. Sometimes Mick the Mouse would sleep inside the box, which they made cosy with some pieces of fluff pulled out of Evil Teddy (his father got in trouble for *that*, too).

One Saturday, SuperBaby's mother left SuperBaby with his father again, so she could go shopping for shoes with Grandma. For some reason, shoe shopping was very important.

'Look after the baby properly this time!' she scolded him. 'Don't let the cat into his room again!'

'But I didn't -'

'And don't hide Green Teddy!' added Grandma.

'I never -'

'And he's sound asleep, so don't
wake him!' said the mother.

'I won't -'

'And don't stick Green Teddy in
the fireplace again,' said Grandma.

'But I -'

Ben Vickery

The mother said, 'And listen outside his door every ten minutes to make sure he's not crying.'

'I will.'

Grandma added, 'I'm going to put this in the bin
outside.' She showed him a small, worn cereal box.

'You can't do that,' said the father. 'That's the baby's special box. He loves it!'

'It's dirty,' said Grandma. 'And it stinks! It smells
like a mouse has been living in it. *And* it's got bits of
green teddy bear fluff inside!' She gave him a suspicious look.

'I didn't -' said the father.

'Oh, yes you did!'

So the father fed the cat, watched television... and
fell asleep in his chair. Meanwhile, SuperBaby woke
and felt around for Ben the Box. He wanted to read

the word Sugar again and practice the bigger words like Dicalcium Phosphate and Niacinamide.

Oh no! Ben the Box was missing!

He cried for a while, but no one came to check on him. So he climbed out of his cot and began searching the room. Still no box!

Cat the Cat scratched at the door, so SuperBaby flew to the doorknob and turned it to let the cat in.

'I've lost Ben the Box!' SuperBaby cried.

'Grandma took him out of your cot,' said Cat the Cat, sitting on Evil Teddy and cleaning a paw.

'Oh no!' exclaimed SuperBaby. 'He's been Box-napped!'

'Worse than that,' said the cat. 'She put him in the rubbish bin on the drive.'

SuperBaby said, 'We must save him!'

'That'll be tricky,' said the cat. 'That bin has a heavy lid.'

'Please will you help me?'

'Of course. Friends always help each other. And afterwards, you can help me open one of those tins of sardines your parents keep in the pantry. I can never get them open by myself,' she mewed.

'It's a deal!'

SuperBaby picked up the cat and flew out the window and down to the bin. Cat the Cat was right: the big black bin had a heavy lid that kept banging shut as he tried to keep it open with one hand while poking about inside it with the other. So Cat the Cat leapt onto the rim of the bin and held it open with her head so that the baby could fly down into the bin and search for Ben the Box.

Neither of them noticed the bin lorry stopping by the house. Neither of them noticed a burly bin man walking up the drive.

'Hey – cat! – get outta there!' shouted the bin man. The cat fell off the bin; the bin lid clanged shut; inside the bin, everything went dark.

Then SuperBaby was bounced about as the bin was rolled along the uneven drive. He tried to cry for help, but he got a mouthful of apple peelings.

'Yummy!' he said.

Then the bin was turned upside down and he was falling, falling, falling… and soon he was underneath a big pile of stinky garbage that was being driven down the road inside a huge bin lorry.

Rocky the Rat

SuperBaby climbed up and sat on the top of the swaying pile of rubbish in the lorry. He thought about crying, but said bravely to himself, 'I must save Ben the Box!'

'Who?' asked a voice next to him.

SuperBaby peered into the garbage. Two beady eyes peered out at him, above a furry nose and long whiskers. A long tail poked out nearby.

'I'm looking for Ben the Box,' said SuperBaby. 'Who are you? Are you a friend of Mick the Mouse?'

'Nah!' said the voice. 'I'm a rat. We don't hang out wiv wimpy mice.'

'What's your name?'

'Rocky.'

'Rocky the Rat!' said SuperBaby with delight. 'You can be my new friend!'

'Charmed, I'm sure,' said Rocky. 'But where's your Box friend gone?'

'I don't know,' said SuperBaby. 'Grandma put Ben the Box in the bin. And now he's in this pile of garbage somewhere. And there's so much of everything here – so I'll *never* find him!'

SuperBaby began to cry, just as any baby would. Rocky the Rat crawled across and patted him kindly on the knee with a scratchy and rather dirty paw.

'There, there,' said the rat. 'Have some chips.'

He pulled forward a soggy bundle of crumpled newspaper and ripped it open to reveal a greasy bag of cold fried potatoes that smelled interesting: tangy and salty with a hint of malt. SuperBaby tried one.

'They're wonderful!' he said and stopped crying immediately. 'I want to eat them forever!'

'Yeah,' said the rat. 'Nuffink like a bag of cold, greasy fries wiv salt an' vinegar. My favourite an' all.'

'There's so much nice food in the world!' exclaimed the baby. 'Have you tried baby food with rice and sugar and milk power and dicalcium phosphate in it?'

'Nah,' said the rat. 'Is it tasty?'

'It's as good as cold chips! It's yummy and sweet!'

'I wish I could try it,' sighed Rocky the Rat.

'You can!' said the baby. 'If you help me find Ben the Box, you can come home with me and I'll share my cereal with you!'

'You got yourself a deal,' said the rat.

'And when we find Ben the Box,' said the baby, 'I can fill him with chips! Hooray!'

'Good idea,' said Rocky. 'And I got me a plan…'

The bin lorry emptied its load at the Waste Centre and drove away. Rocky tunnelled his way out of the pile of rubbish, with SuperBaby following. He gave a sharp rat squeak and all his mates came running.

Soon, hundreds of rats were searching through the garbage, looking for a blue and red box about the size of a rat, with a picture of a happy baby on it. Ten minutes later, a delighted SuperBaby was hugging his box and Rocky was loading it with chips.

'Will you come live at my house?' SuperBaby

asked. 'I have a big cupboard full of cuddly toys and you can hide inside it!'

'Nah,' said Rocky. 'Humans get bovvered if rats move in. I'll come visit, though. And I'll teach ya how to whistle a Rat Call whenever you need me!'

They flew back to the baby's house, SuperBaby holding the box under one arm and the rat under the other. He got into his cot and – being suddenly very tired – fell sound asleep.

When his mother came home shortly after this, she asked the father, 'Has the baby been okay?'

'Yes,' said his father. 'He hasn't made a sound.'

They went upstairs to check on the baby. There he was in his cot, hugging a box with one arm and something furry with the other.

'I thought Grandma threw that box away!' said the mother. 'Did you take it out of the dustbin?'

'I didn't!'

'And what's he chewing on? I smell chips! Did you feed him chips?'

'I didn't!'

'But he's got some chips in his hand! And where did that rat toy come from? Have you hidden Green

Teddy again?'

'But I –'

'His face is dirty! His hands too! Why can't you look after him properly?'

'But I -'

'Shh! You'll wake him!'

They tiptoed away while the baby smiled in his sleep, dreaming of cold greasy chips.

Rick the Brick

Your first toy is very important to you, even if it's only a brick you found at the local park. SuperBaby had been taken there and placed on the lovely warm grass to enjoy the July sunshine.

He saw a caterpillar being attacked by a wasp and nearly flew off to save it, but stopped himself and pretended to be learning to crawl instead.

But he needed to save the caterpillar! Now was the time to practice his latest superpower. He gathered a mouthful of spit and…

Zap! That wasp didn't know what hit it! One moment it was chasing a caterpillar; now it was lying on its back waggling its legs, covered in baby spit.

Meanwhile, SuperBaby's father had found an old red brick with lots of pretty moss on its top edge, like green hair. He took a wax crayon from the toy bag and drew a face on the brick. He set it up on end: and it fell onto its face, making SuperBaby laugh. He set it up again: it fell onto its back. SuperBaby roared with laughter. Then his father made it fall sideways onto his mother's toes, which was even funnier - though his mother didn't think so.

SuperBaby insisted on taking Rick the Brick home with him. As they were walking out of the park they passed the boy from next door, who was throwing sticks at the ducks in the pond...

He had to save the ducks! This was a job for SuperBaby!

But he couldn't sneak away and rescue them, because he was in the stroller. He thought about throwing Rick the Brick, but that would really hurt!

Aha! He had his dummy! He flung the dummy with

all his might.

'Ouch!' the boy shouted as the dummy bounced off his head; but he kept throwing sticks.

Bother. Baby spit time! SuperBaby gathered a mouthful… *Pow!*

Oops… A man jogging along the path brushed past them and got hit instead. Right on the bum.

'Yow!' The jogger looked back at SuperBaby's parents and shook his finger at them.

Bother again. He needed another way to stop the boy. Throw a baby shoe? It might get lost in the pond! He looked at the bags hanging on the pushchair. Baby lotion? Evil teddy? *Yes!*

He cried and pointed at one of the bags until they stopped and offered him things from it.

'Awww. He wants Green Teddy!' said his mother to his father. 'I told you he would like it eventually!'

She gave him the teddy and they continued on their way. A few seconds later they heard an "Ouch!" and a big splash from the pond as the teddy bounced off the boy's head.

Result! No more Evil Teddy!

But the boy was *still* throwing sticks. SuperBaby

looked at the other bags and had a great idea.

Yes! But his parents might notice… so he needed to get them to look away. So he cried again and his parents stopped. He pointed at the ground this time.

'He's lost his dummy,' said his father. He started searching in the path and grass nearby. SuperBaby cried harder, and now his mother started searching as well. While they were busy, the baby felt about in the plastic bag for the dirty nappy his mother had put there a few minutes ago… untaped it… and threw it like a flying saucer….

'Aiiiiii! Help! Help!' screamed the boy as he ran home with another nappy on his head.

Enemies

NO GAMES!
NO DOGS!

Dear Dairy

Yesterday I saw Mummy writing in a little book called Baby's Dairy. I don't agree with some things she wrote so I'm going write Baby's Real Dairy.

I love being with my family and playing games with my friends. I am NOT a difficult baby and Mummy should not write that in her Dairy. I only cry when I get sad or scared or bored or lonely or hungry or need changing or... well, maybe I DO cry a lot but it's a Baby Thing.

Life is good! I love my friends! But I'm worried that I've got some Enemies as well now.

Why doesn't everybody love me? It makes me sad that some people don't like babies. It makes me sadder that they don't like ME. It makes me even sadderer that they make angry faces at me, so I cry.

I like EVERYONE. I like Aunt Sissy who smells of dog wee, Aunt Bessy who wears scary purple lipstick and big scary hats, Uncle Charlie who smokes stinky cigars and sometimes forgets to wash properly. I LOVE my Grandmas and Grandpas and Mummy and Daddy. I think I would even like the boy next door if he would stop throwing things and play with me instead.

Everyone ought to like me back. I'm such a nice baby and I'm NOT difficult!

But not everybody likes babies.

SuperBaby learned this sad fact a few weeks after he'd made friends with Rocky the Rat. He was five months old now and his mother was taking him for a walk; well, *she* was walking, and SuperBaby was just lying on his back in the pram, trying to decide where he could hide Evil Teddy next. Grandma had found the bear floating in the park pond last week, and now it was sharing his pram.

He was watching the blue sky and white fleecy clouds while burbling cute little nonsense sounds as babies do, mixed in with reminders to himself about how to act like a baby.

'Gah gah goo goo!' *I can sit up now but I mustn't try to stand. I'm not quite old enough to do that: I mustn't scare Mummy!* 'Bah burble wurble burger.' *I wonder what a burger tastes like? Rocky says he'll bring me one.* 'Oogle boogle.' *No, don't ask Mummy about burgers. And don't do a cartwheel out of the pram. And don't start talking to Mick the Mouse, even though he's being a bit tickly.'*

Mick had panicked when SuperBaby's mother came to take the baby from his cot, and had dived inside SuperBaby's romper suit, thinking that was a good place to hide. If SuperBaby's mother had looked closely, she would have seen a mouse-sized lump under SuperBaby's left armpit.

They crossed the road. SuperBaby smiled. They were going to pass by the people who lived across the road – the ones who shook their garden shears and fists at him whenever he flew past. That must be their way of saying they wanted to be friends!

SuperBaby's mother paused at the gate to gaze at the big house and perfect garden. She lifted SuperBaby from the pram to look. 'Look at the lovely garden, baby!' she whispered. 'Maybe one day we'll have a garden as big and perfect as this one!'

The house was the biggest in the road. It was painted pale blue with white windows, and had a tidy garden around it. The grass was exactly one centimetre high and the edges of the lawn were sharp and straight. Every tree and shrub was trimmed to perfection. The roses were like a picture and the green glossy leaves on the rosebushes looked like they had been polished. There were no weeds.

His mother waved to the couple, who were spraying some nasty-smelling chemicals onto the plants.

The plant spray made SuperBaby cough, and his eyes were stinging. (You might know that children are more sensitive to chemicals than adults, and babies are the most sensitive of all. There are plenty of sprays and powders that your parents hardly notice, but which can make *you* very sick indeed.)

SuperBaby's mother called to them, 'Hi, what a pretty garden you have. Mine is full of weeds!'

The couple glided across to the fence, carrying their containers full of foul-smelling liquids. They were wearing matching green wax coats, smart trousers, green gloves and green wellington boots.

They smiled at SuperBaby's mother, but not at SuperBaby. The man said, 'You need to get rid of *your* weeds before they infect *our* garden. You should be like us! *Kill them all!*'

The woman added (they seemed to take turns talking), 'We spray them and wipe them out! They don't dare raise their horrid little weed heads here: they know we'll kill them again!'

'And we kill all the bugs too. I've got the bug spray here on my back...'

'... We hate them! Nasty woodlice and beetles and centipedes and millipedes...'

'... Slugs and snails and ants...'

'... Spiders and flies and wasps and bees.'

SuperBaby's mother exclaimed, 'Oh, but I like most of those!'

The man frowned and pointed his bug sprayer at her. 'That's why you have nasty bugs everywhere...'

'... Holes in your apples...'

'... Black spots on your rose bushes...'

'... Weevils and stinkbugs and caterpillars...'

'... Ladybirds and their weird larvae...'

'... So you have to kill them all!'

'... You must have no pity!'

'... No mercy!'

'... *Slaughter them!*'

SuperBaby's mother looked rather surprised about all the killing that was going on just across the road.

She said, 'Oh… that must take a lot of work.'

The couple looked at each other and nodded together. The man said, 'The nasty little creatures keep coming back, so we have to keep killing them. They get in from the houses next door…'

'… And from across the road. Lots of them sneak across from your house!'

They looked at each other and nodded again.

'We have to set traps for the *big* pests too…'

'… Dirty rats and mice and sly squirrels and greedy pigeons and grass snakes and slow worms…'

'… And we've got traps for bothersome cats. Your cat had better watch out! It comes here - '

'- into *our* garden!'

'- trying to catch the birds.'

SuperBaby's mother said, 'I'm sorry about that. But you know what cats are like.'

'Yeah. They're Bad. Like babies.'

'Babies?' SuperBaby's mother was truly shocked now. SuperBaby was shocked too, and began to cry.

The couple looked at him, then looked at each other and nodded again. 'That's a very noisy baby!' they both said at the same time.

'Your baby kept us awake last night…'

'… He often does that!'

'… He was crying very loud. You should keep his window shut tight and teach him some manners…'

'… He was crying this morning, too. This used to be such a quiet neighbourhood. *Now* there's noisy babies and noisy cats and noisy birds.'

SuperBaby's mother said, 'Well, they can't help it, can they? All babies cry.'

The man said, 'They should respect their neighbours. Their parents should teach them that!'

The woman said, 'We're very reasonable people. But some noises are *totally unacceptable:* like your baby's crying. And he laughs very loud as well.'

The man added, 'Noisy children are a *nuisance*. All that running about and crying and laughing and shouting and giggling. It shouldn't be allowed!'

The woman said, 'And there's a big, black mother crow that shouts rude crow noises down our chimney. She does it on purpose. Like your baby does.'

The man added, 'And you shouldn't let your baby wander about bothering people. Babies should be unseen and unheard.'

SuperBaby's mother was puzzled and asked, 'Wandering around? But he spends most of the day sleeping in his cot!'

The couple nodded at one another yet again.

'He sits on that window ledge over there…'

'… And he flies about like one of those scary vampire bats…'

'… Drops that green teddy bear in the ditch…'

'… Hangs it on lamp posts…'

'… You shouldn't let him do that….'

They said in chorus: *'You're a bad mother!'*

SuperBaby's mother said, 'I'm sure you've mistaken. He's just a baby.'

The woman said, 'We saw him! He even dropped his nappy in your next door neighbour's garden!'

'He'd better not do that in *our* garden …'

'… Yeah, we'll get a baby trap!'

'… *Snap!*'

'… *Crunch!*'

'… *Gotcha!*'

SuperBaby was crying in earnest now. *They didn't like him! And they were going to catch him in a baby trap!*

The couple turned to each other once more and

said, 'He's doing it again!'

'... And that's *our* bit of pavement he's crying on!'

'... It shouldn't be allowed!'

'... They come into our country and take our jobs and cry on our pavements...'

'... And they drop their nappies everywhere!'

SuperBaby's mother turned away to put SuperBaby back into the pram. But something had wriggled out of SuperBaby's romper suit, then dropped to the ground and run onto the grass: something small and shy and timid, but also very, very angry.

'*A mouse!*' the couple shouted.

'*Squeak squeak squeakety squeak!*' Mick the Mouse scolded them. '*Squeak squeak squeakety –!*'

Then he had to dodge to one side, because the man tried to stomp on him with a big green boot.

The woman tried to kick the mouse, but missed and kicked her husband instead.

The man hopped around on one leg and nearly squashed Mick, who leapt away and landed on the lady's boot.

She screeched and tried to shake him off. Mick panicked and bit a hole in the boot. She flicked him up into the air and he landed on the man's head. The man tried to hit Mick with the hand holding the bug spray handle, but he poked the nozzle into his own ear instead and filled it with bug spray.

The woman swung at Mick with a garden trowel but missed, and the mud in the trowel flew into the man's other ear. The man shook his head violently to get the bug spray out of one ear and mud out of the other, and Mick slipped off the head.

The mouse slid down the green jacket, trying to hold onto the waxy material with his sharp claws, while the woman bashed at him with her garden hand trowel, missing him each time but whacking her husband rather successfully.

Mick slid onto the green trousers, which was very painful to the man because his wife was following Mick's course with misplaced trowel thumps. The mouse slid to the top of one of the man's boot… teetered on the edge… and fell inside the boot.

The man was hopping up and down on one leg now, while his wife laid into his legs with the trowel. He kicked his boot off. It turned over twice in the air, bounced off his head, and landed in a rose bush.

'Ha ha!' he cried as he snatched the boot from the rose bush and crushed the top shut. 'Got you!'

He banged the boot on the ground several times. Then he stuck the sprayer nozzle into the top and started filling it with bug spray. He crowed, 'You won't be bothering us again, you little –'

'*Squeak!*' called something from the rose bush. Mick poked his head out from between some flowers. '*Na-na-na-na squeak!*' he called and leaped down.

The man looked sadly at the ruined boot in his hand. He shook his fist at Mick as the little mouse scampered across the lawn, squeezed under the gate and ran after the pram.

SuperBaby's mother was marching away with her head held high, pushing the pram at great speed while muttering rude things about the gardening couple. Mick didn't catch up with them until they stopped at the corner before crossing another road. He waited until SuperBaby's mother was looking the other way, then scrambled up into the pram.

'That was very naughty,' SuperBaby whispered to Mick. 'But it was also very funny!'

When SuperBaby returned home, he planned to warn Cat the Cat about the people opposite. But he fell asleep instead… and when he woke later that day, he forgot all about it because it was Milk Time! He loved milk! He drank his milk, burped, and took his tiny book and pencil from the cupboard…

Dear Baby's Real Dairy

What are fathers for? Mothers give you lovely sweet warm milk and also give you lovely sweet warm smiles while you drink it. They say gentle things and sing to you. They do most of the dressing and nappy changing, too.

My father disappears every morning and isn't around when I need him to play with me after I've read a book from the shelf in my room. He doesn't do half the things on the Lists that Mummy gives him. And when he changes my nappy he looks worried, like he's afraid it might explode!

I've decided to turn my first enemies into friends and will ask my three friends how to do it. Four if you include Ben the Box, but he doesn't say much.

P.S. Mummy spells Dairy wrong.

'It's easy!' SuperBaby said when they had gathered in his room the next morning. 'I'll give the funny people across the road some nice things. Then they'll like me and become my friends!'

Cat the Cat paused from cleaning her face with a paw and asked, 'You'll give them bits of fish?'

'*Squeak?*' asked Mick.

'I think that means *cheese*,' said the cat.

'Yeah,' said Rocky. 'But I expect they'd like cold greasy chips even better.'

'That's a great idea!' said SuperBaby.

The next morning, he got some special presents together and flew them into the pram while his mother was busy finding her shoes.

They went for a walk most days now and they usually crossed the road by their own front gate, because that was the shortest way to the park.

SuperBaby couldn't see the people across the road because he was always lying on his back or else sitting in his pram looking at his mother. He wouldn't know until his mother turned onto the pavement opposite whether the Enemies were near.

This time he was lucky: they were snapping their

cutters at some tiny branches that were out of place on the tidy hedge next to the gate.

His mother turned her head and said 'Hello!' as they passed. SuperBaby knew that he probably wasn't quite old enough to wave, so he waved at them while his mother wasn't looking.

They didn't wave back because they were still his Enemies. *That wouldn't last long, though! They were going to be his friends!* They did pause from their clipping and chopping for a moment, and muttered something.

SuperBaby knew he definitely wasn't old enough to say words, so he made a *'Bahboodlegabble!'* noise at them instead. Unfortunately, because he had just had a lot of milk, it ended with a big BURP.

They glared at him, then looked at each other and said firmly: '*Such* bad manners!'

He had upset them again! Oh well, he would soon put that right. Time for presents!

He waited until his mother was looking away, then flung his presents out of the pram. They disappeared over the hedge and he was pleased to hear the couple exclaim with surprise at the flying goodies.

They were going to be so pleased!

'What was that?' he heard the woman say.

'Nearly took my head off!' the man replied.

'On the grass – look there!'

'A tin of sardines?'

'And a lump of cheese.'

'A greasy bag of… chips??'

'And one of those things a baby sucks!'

'Not a new one either!'

SuperBaby smiled. *They would be his friends now! He'd given them some treats and his second favourite dummy!*

Then the presents came flying back over the fence and bounced onto the road.

Oh well. He would try again tomorrow…

The next day, he sent them things he'd heard his aunts say were "good for you": a bit of broccoli, a tomato and a dictionary… and Green Teddy. *Hooray! No more Evil Teddy!* But these came back as well.

After that he tried a few things that Daddy liked. They held onto the bag of crisps and the marshmallows, but they threw back the slice of bacon. Maybe he should have cooked it first?

For the next week, he tried all manner of tasty

food; but it never seemed right. The people still looked angry with him! When he waved, they waved their cutting, chopping or spraying things back at him: but not in a happy way.

He didn't give up. He waved harder! And whenever his mother crossed the road and walked past their gate, he gave them a SuperBaby *Gahgah-googoo!* and usually a SuperBurp as well!

He held another meeting with his friends. After sharing a tin of sardines and cheese with them, he asked what he could try next.

'*Squeak!*'

'I think he's saying cheese again,' said the Cat. 'But they don't want cheese. They don't even want sardines. They must be crazy!'

Rocky said, 'You gotta remember that humans have funny tastes. They throw away all the nice, stinky bits of food we rats like so much. You gotta give 'em what they like, even if it don't make sense.'

SuperBaby thought hard. 'They like killing bugs.'

Cat the Cat said, 'So give them some bugs to kill.'

'Oh. I hadn't thought of that!'

So for the next week, he tried flicking woodlice

and slugs and other small garden pests over the hedgerow. But he still didn't get a friendly smile.

Finally he had a brilliant thought: *They liked plants!* It was so simple! Give them plants!

So one evening, as soon as his parents turned off their bedroom light, he zoomed into the shed in the back garden and collected all the packets of seeds he could find. He also found the small garden digger thing his parents used for the tubs of flowers on the patio. Then he flew across the road with these.

It took him a whole hour to dig twenty-five holes around the garden and plant the seeds in them. Surely now they would be happy with him!

The next morning, he was very excited as his mother crossed the road and turned onto the pavement. As the pram turned, his heart leaped: the people were waiting for them at the gate!

He made great burbling baby sounds at them and smiled. They didn't smile back.

The man held up something that flashed in the morning light. 'I think this might be your hand trowel?' he asked SuperBaby's mother.

She stopped. 'Mine? Why do you say that?'

'Look!' The man turned the garden trowel around so that she could read her name written in black ink on the handle.

'Oh,' she said. 'Why do you have it?'

'You tell me,' said the man.

'Yes, tell us!' said his wife. 'Tell us about the holes in the lawn!'

'… And the tin of sardines!'

'… The bag of marshmallows!'

'… The broccoli! The scary green teddy bear!'

'… The jar of chocolate spread!'

'… That was quite nice, actually… '

'… Shame it was followed by an invasion of wood-lice and slugs…'

'… And centipedes and millipedes and earwigs!'

SuperBaby's mother took the garden trowel from them and looked at it, puzzled. 'Somebody must have taken this from our garden,' she said. 'Why would they do that?'

The man and woman looked at each other and nodded slowly.

'We know who it was,' said the man.

'... And he's a very naughty baby!'

'... Him and that bad cat that's always with him!'

'... So the next time they bother us – Snap!'

'... Crunch!'

'... Gotcha!'

They each pointed a finger at the pram.

Two days later, SuperBaby woke in the middle of the night because Mick the Mouse was squeaking in his ear. He sat up in his cot and tried to focus his eyes on the small creature.

'What's wrong, Mick?'

'Squeakety squeak-squeak! SqueAk sQueaK squeak-eek!'

SuperBaby shook his head. 'I don't understand you,' he said.

Mick thought about this. Then he pointed at the window with a mouse claw.

'You want to go out?'

'Squeak!' A shake of the head.

'You don't. Okay. You want the window open?'

'Squeak!' Another shake.

'Closed?'

'*Squeak!*'

Mick pointed at himself. Then he shook his head.

'You aren't Mick?'

'*Squeakity squeak!*'

'Okay. You *are* Mick.'

'*Squeak!*' Mick held his paws to his face and turned his claws outwards.

'Oh! You wish you had bigger whiskers!'

'*Squeak!*' Mick folded his ears to make them come to a point.

'You… don't like your ears either.'

'*Squeak!*' Mick thought hard, then licked a paw and pretended to wash his face, like a cat.

'You're being Cat the Cat!' SuperBaby exclaimed, clapping his hands.

'*Duh!*' Mick replied. Then he climbed onto the top bar of the cot and washed his face again. He pointed at the window once more.

'I understand now!' said SuperBaby. 'Cat the Cat went out the window!'

'*Squeak…*'

'Oh. She didn't?'

'*Squeak!*' Mick pointed further.

'Oh. She went… into the front garden…'

'Squeak…' (And a mouse nod).

'Out through the gate…'

'Squeak…' Another nod.

'Across the road?'

'Squeak…' Vigorous nodding.

'Uh oh! Did she go into the scary garden?'

Mick nodded solemnly. Then he pretended to snatch something up and throw it into the cot.

SuperBaby shouted, 'They've caught Cat the Cat! Oh no!'

There were running footsteps along the hallway and the sound of the doorknob being turned. SuperBaby dived under the covers and Mick dived with him. When his father peered in at him, the moonlight from the window showed the baby fast asleep, hugging a small cuddly toy.

'He must have been calling out in a dream,' yawned the father as he climbed back into his bed.

'But it sounded like words!' said the mother.

'We must have imagined them. By the way, he really loves his little mouse toy.'

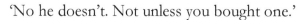

'He doesn't have a mouse toy.'

'Yes he does.'

'No he doesn't. Not unless you bought one.'

'Grandma must have bought it.'

'You probably imagined it.'

SuperBaby waited several minutes, then crept out of his bed and listened at his parents' door. They were asleep.

He dashed back to his room and put on his black baby suit and black knitted baby cap. He didn't want anybody to see him this time. Then as he flew to the window, he saw his reflection: he needed to cover his face! But what could he use?

He flew down to the kitchen and searched the shelves. Tomato ketchup? Peanut butter? No – *There it was!* The perfect way to disguise himself!!

He took the big jar of chocolate spread back to his room and spread some on his face. Then he licked his fingers… and licked the lid… and hid the jar in the back of his wardrobe.

'I might need it again,' he explained to Mick.

'*Squeak!*' agreed Mick, who was licking at any chocolate on SuperBaby's face that he could reach from his perch on SuperBaby's shoulder.

SuperBaby opened his window and paused on the window ledge. 'SuperBaby to the rescue!' he cried.

'*Squeak!*' agreed Mick.

They flew high, keeping well away from the street lights. Then SuperBaby spiralled down over the house across the road and landed on its chimney.

He looked all around. Dark shadow lay upon the grassy lawns that surrounded the house. A hazy moon and the distant street lights picked out the perfect flower beds and the carefully trimmed dark shrubs dotted about - and all the untidy blobs on the grass where SuperBaby had tried to turn his enemies into friends by planting flower seeds for them.

There was also a beautiful circular shed behind the house, with its door propped open. Mick was pointing in that direction.

'*Squeak...*' he whispered.

SuperBaby flew down carefully and landed on the top edge of the open door. He leaned forward and peered into the darkness of the shed. He could see only dark blobs and darker blobs. He smelled something fishy.

'Cat?' he whispered.

There came back a noise that might have been a low growl, or might have been quiet laughter. He dropped to the ground and crept into the shed on his hands and knees.

The fishy smell was stronger now. He followed the scent to his left and up onto a wooden bench. He felt forward with his hand…

Snap!

It was a mouse trap! SuperBaby had snatched away his fingers just in time!

'Squeakity ouch!' said a tiny, frightened voice from his shoulder.

SuperBaby thought to himself, *'I should have brought one of those light things you can switch on. I'll just have to wait until my eyes adjust to the light in here.'*

And then the door was slammed shut, and suddenly it was as dark as… as dark as… as dark as the inside of a shed with no windows.

'Bother!' exclaimed SuperBaby.

'*Squeak!*' added Mick.

'Meow?' asked another voice, which sounded weak and rather sad.

'Cat the Cat?' asked SuperBaby, looking around in the darkness (which didn't help much).

'*Squeak?*' asked Mick, tilting his head to one side and listening (which helped more).

'Meow. I don't feel well,' said the weak voice. 'I think I ate too many sardines. And I don't think they were good sardines… '

'Where are you?'

'Meowwww. I'm inside a box somewhere. I was eating sardines somebody had left in it, and I felt sick and fell over and can't get out. Oh yuk… I'll never eat sardines again! Yowwwww….'

SuperBaby bumped into an open wooden box on the floor. He felt about inside it cautiously. There was a warm, furry animal at the bottom.

'*Squeak?*' asked the voice from his shoulder.

'I'm all right, Mick,' said the cat. 'But I feel very, very ill. Can we go home now?'

'I don't know how to open the door,' said SuperBaby. 'It closed itself. Maybe it's locked.'

He went to investigate and pushed hard at the door. 'It's stuck,' he said.

'We're caught!' groaned the cat. 'We're stuck in here *forever!*'

'*Squeakkkkk… eekity squeak,*' moaned the mouse from SuperBaby's shoulder.

'Haha!' said a different voice from outside the shed. 'Got them all!'

'Shhhhh! Not so loud!' whispered the wife of the first voice.

'Who cares?' he whispered back. 'It's the baby and his weird pets. I'm not afraid of them!'

'… A *flying* baby!'

'… We're going to be rich, rich, rich!'

'… Did you check the video?'

'Of course. Night setting. Perfect recording. Even did a bit of slow motion part way through.'

'… We'll be rich!'

'… Sell it to the papers -'

'… No! The government!'

'… No! A *foreign* government!'

'… Russia!'

'… North Korea!'

'… Maybe even the USA!'

'… Or whoever pays us the most!'

' We can buy a bigger house…'

'… With an enormous garden… '

'… All those weeds to kill!'

'… And the insects! We can slaughter millions!'

'… Billions!'

'… Trillions!'

They both sighed deeply.

'We'll have a perfect house with the biggest, tidiest, weed-free, bug-free grounds in England!'

'Maybe the biggest in the world!'

'We're so clever!' the woman exclaimed.

The man said calmly, 'We are, my dear. Now, let's make our plans carefully. We mustn't slip up at the last moment.'

'Check the video camera,' she said.

'All perfect, my darling. Good film of the little monster flying across. Great footage of him circling the garden.'

'Check the shed.'

'All locked and secure. A gorilla would have trouble escaping.'

'Maybe one last video when we let him out tomorrow at dawn?'

'What a good idea! You are a treasure! But… Do we *want* to let him out?'

'Oooooo! We could sell him to the scientists!'

'The Space Agency!'

'Or Disney World!'

'No, that would be wrong.'

They both sighed again, deeply and sadly.

'We'll have to let him go this time. But *we know where he lives!*'

'And knowledge is power, my precious.'

'And power is money, my little cupcake!'

'Ha ha!'

The man became serious again. 'But we need to deal with the Pet Pests.'

'… The bad cat.'

'… The boot-biting mouse.'

'Yes. Let's make a plan…'

SuperBaby had heard enough. He thought it might be fun to go to Disney World, but he wasn't going to let his friends be *"dealt with"!*

'Hang on tight, both of you!' he called to his friends, putting Mick on his shoulder and clasping Cat the Cat to his chest. He flew around the hut and felt about quietly. There were no windows, and the door and walls seemed to be strong. He reached above him and felt how the roof came to a point, like a big witch's hat.

He pushed upwards. The roof creaked a little. He knew he wasn't strong enough yet to do really powerful things, but maybe he could push his way through the peak of the roof.

He took a firmer hold of Cat the Cat with his left hand and put his right hand on the wood at the very top of the shed roof.

'SuperBaby to the rescue!' he cried.

'Squeak!'

'Meow!'

He pushed as hard as he could. Oh, this was tough! The shed refused to budge. But he had to do it! He *had* to save his friends!

He gritted his baby teeth and pushed with all his baby might. The whole shed began to shake. Then it began to rise in the air.

Outside, the gardening couple were still exclaiming about their coming wealth.

'I think we'll have a yacht.'

'… Why not two?'

'… And a sports car each.'

'… And – *What's going on?*'

'Quick! Get the camera ready!'

'Switched on. Focused. Night action setting. Oh, we'll make millions from this!'

The shed rose a few metres, shaking. It looked like a space rocket rising slowly from its launch pad, fighting against gravity. Then the nails holding the nose cone of the roof to the rocket body of the shed began to give way.

'Look! How exciting!' said the people outside. 'It's separating!'

The main body of the shed fell back into its original place with a thump. The cone, freed from its restraint, shot upwards suddenly.

'Keep filming!' shouted the woman.

The cone spiralled upwards. Everyone in it was feeling very dizzy. SuperBaby didn't know which direction he was going.

'Which way is our house?' he whispered.

'Which was is *up?*' Cat the Cat mewed back.

While SuperBaby was thinking about this, his grip on the wooden supports slipped. The cone roof tilted suddenly and he couldn't hold it.

Down below, a video camera was recording the erratic path of the spinning shed roof.

'Zoom in on the baby!' said a female voice.

'Where is he?' her husband replied.

'Give the camera to me!' She snatched it.

'Give it back! You're useless with a camera!'

'I'm better than you are!'

The video camera zoomed in on a baby trying to hold a shed roof upright. The roof wobbled, slipped, turned upside and began to fall to the ground.

Two people looked up in horror.

'It's right above us!'

'It's going to squash us!'

'Run! That way!'

'No! *That* way!'

'That's the wrong way!'

'Move!'

'No! *You* move!'

'Keep filming!'

'*You* keep filming!'

They both pushed the camera into each other's hands and ran in opposite directions.

The camera dropped to the ground. They

fled left and right. The shed roof, its cone pointed downwards, dropped like a stone. Its sharp peak landed on the discarded video camera, smashing it deep into the grassy earth.

Two people walked back across the lawn and looked down at the smashed roof and the ruined grass and flower bed and camera. Then they looked up at the dizzy creatures hovering above them.

In the cool, moist night, half-lit by the hazy moon and distant stars, a baby and two animals were still slowly spinning. SuperBaby finally managed to pause in mid-air and looked around, trying to get his bearings. He looked down at the garden.

'There's somebody down there!' SuperBaby whispered to his friends.

'I don't feel well,' groaned the Cat. 'In fact, I think I'm going to be very, very sick. Oh meow yuk… Oh yowl urrrrrrkkkkk…'

'Uh oh,' said SuperBaby. 'I think the people down there just got covered…'

'*Squeak! Gotcha!*'

Babysitters

Dear Baby's Real Dairy

I expect that everyone remembers the first time they got stuck on the ceiling. I remember it as if it was last week. Because it was.

When I was five months old my parents started leaving me with babysitters. Grandma is my favourite because she gives me lots of cuddles and tiny bits of chocolate. She always whispers Don't Tell Anybody! when she gives me chocolate and once I accidentally whispered back I Won't! Fortunately she didn't hear me.

Grandpa always plays funny games and then falls asleep in a chair so I have to get my own chocolate from the top shelf in the kitchen.

Those are the good sitters. There are some less good ones. Aunt Sissy has four dogs and is always coated with little white dog hairs and smells faintly of dog wee. Aunt Bessy sings weird lullabies. Uncle Charles doesn't like changing nappies and leaves them until they're dripping. And as for Mad Mary, the teenager from down the road...

Everyone calls her Mary but I know her real name. She is definitely Mad Mary. She is mad at everybody and she is crazy.

SuperBaby first met Mad Mary her when his parents visited her parents. She was bouncing on a trampoline while shouting into her phone. Their second meeting was when they passed her in the park, lying on the grass shouting into her phone.

After that, they met quite often and each time she had a phone in her hand. Sometimes she shouted at it, sometimes she poked at it in an annoyed way, and sometimes she was waving it at a friend and shouting at them instead.

When SuperBaby learned that his parents were planning to leave him with Mad Mary, he knew he would have to use all his baby skills on her: cute gurgles, tears, howls, laughs, snuffles and whimpers - with every baby wave, kick, smile, frown and wiggle he knew. He spent an hour practising them before she came.

All babies do this. They have to find the best way to get what they want. It's like pressing random buttons on a mobile phone or TV controller to see what happens.

SuperBaby's parents did all the right things to make him feel happy about being left with someone new. They put him in his tiny bouncy chair in the front room and gave him a baby book to look at and a toy to play with. Then they brought Mad Mary to see him and told him:

'You're such a lucky boy! Mary's going to look after you for a few hours. She's going to play with you and give you a bottle of milk and sing songs to you!'

Mad Mary looked up from her phone, smiled brightly at SuperBaby and said, 'What fun!'

'Gah gah goo goo!' SuperBaby said excitedly, kicking his little legs.

His parents gave him big hugs and left him with Mary, who watched out the window until they drove away. Then she sat on the sofa and poked about on her phone while he studied her from his tiny bouncy chair in the front room.

He spread his arms wide and put a big smile on his face. He did some chuckles and *ba-ba-ba* noises to warm up, then gave her a sweet gurgling laugh that would have melted the heart of a vampire.

It didn't work.

Mad Mary just frowned at him and went back to playing a game on her phone.

He tried the gurgle that means "Please play with me!" She poked at her phone some more.

He tried the "I love you!" gurgle. She turned her back on him.

This was serious. He tried crying instead.

That got her attention! She walked right across to him… walked past him… then pulled some headphones out of her bag and put them over her ears.

He cried louder. She turned up the volume of her music. He cried louder still.

Result! She stood up and hurried over to his baby chair. She was going to pick him up!

No she wasn't… She just moved his chair into a far corner and went back to sit on the sofa.

Okay, this was war. Tantrum Time!

He kicked his legs and howled. He made sad blubbery noises and angry screeching noises.

She ignored him - for half an hour! She listened to music and played on her phone instead.

Finally she got up and came to him. He held up his little arms to her, tiny tears running down his cheeks.

'Look, baby!' she said sternly. 'I've got better things to do than play with you. Your mum and dad would have to pay me a lot more money if they want me to bother with *that*.'

She held up three fingers. 'Here's the deal: you get one feed, one nappy change, and then you go to bed. So you can cry all you like. You can cry for an hour and then you'll be so tired with crying that you'll fall asleep, and I'll put you in your cot - *without dinner.*'

SuperBaby stopped crying and thought about this.

She continued, 'Or you can stop crying now, and I'll still put you to bed after an hour, but at least you'll get your bottle first. Doesn't bother me either way: I've got my earphones.'

SuperBaby blew a raspberry at her. It wasn't fair!

'Stopped crying, have we? Then let's go outside for a few minutes. I need a cigarette.'

Mad Mary pulled him out of his chair and carried him out to the garden. It was about 8 o'clock, with the sun going down. She set him down on the grass and sat on a low garden recliner. She reached into a pocket and took out a packet of cigarettes and a lighter, which she put down on the little garden side table next to her.

'Don't tell your parents about this,' she laughed. She picked up the lighter.

'Oh no! Smoking is bad for you!' thought SuperBaby. His mother said that smoking killed people. He didn't want Mad Mary to die, even if she was crazy and mean. What would his parents say if they came

home to a dead babysitter in the garden? And maybe he would be blamed for it, and the police would arrest him and lock him up in Baby Prison!

Mad Mary put a cigarette in her mouth and flicked the lighter. A flame spurted. She moved it towards the cigarette.

SuperBaby blew it out. One tiny super-puff and *Zap! No flame!* (He held one hand to the side of his face to hide what he was doing).

Mary gave the lighter a puzzled look. She flicked it again. Flame again.

SuperBaby blew it out again.

Mary put her cigarette down on the side table and studied the lighter. She played with the flame. It seemed okay. She reached for the cigarette. SuperBaby blew again. The cigarette rolled away from her. She grabbed at it, but too late! It flew off the table and disappeared across the grass into the nettles at the edge of the back garden.

Mad Mary looked at her right hand, which had been pointed towards the flying cigarette. 'Did I do that?' she asked.

She turned her hand towards the packet of cigarettes. With one baby puff, the packet began to slide across the table. She had to grab it quickly.

'Wow. Didn't know I could do that.'

She needed a hand free to take out another cigarette, so she put the lighter down.

'Don't you move!' she said to the lighter. She pointed at it.

SuperBaby blew the lighter off the table.

'What the – ?'

Just then the boy next door clambered up the wooden fence and put his head over the top. 'Naa naa nuh NAA naa!' he shouted.

'Get down off that fence, you little toad!' Mad Mary shouted back.

SuperBaby blew at the boy. He couldn't knock him off with a super puff, but he did manage to blow the boy's hair about. He needed a better weapon…

'Can't make me!' the boy shouted.

'Can't I?' Mad Mary pointed her finger at him.

SuperBaby flicked a bogey at the boy. It hit him right in the middle of the forehead. The boy fell backwards off the fence.

'Owwwwww! You shot me! I'm gonna tell my

Mum!' he howled as he ran away.

Mad Mary stared at her pointing finger. 'That's amazing!' she breathed. 'I didn't know I could do that! Wait'll I get home and show the family! They ain't gonna boss *me* around no more! Yeah – I'm gonna say to 'em Take *that*, you mouthy, mangy bunch of losers! You don't mess with Mary! Cos this is what'll happen to you!'

She dropped the packet of cigarettes onto the table and pointed at it again. SuperBaby giggled and blew the packet so hard that it flew across the lawn and hit the fence.

Mad Mary kissed her finger. 'Wow! I'm *incredible!* That Sonia, she's gonna be real sorry she called me a cow at school last week. And my mum had better not ask me to do the washing up when I'm busy on the phone. I'll zap her right across the kitchen!'

She picked up SuperBaby and carried him back to his little chair in the front room.

'You stay here. I'm going upstairs where it's quiet so I can phone my boyfriend and tell him the news about my New Powers. See you in half an hour!'

She went away, leaving a sad and puzzled SuperBaby kicking his heels. He wanted to play a game. That's what babysitters were for: games, cuddles and sometimes sweets!

Then he smiled. He could play the special game that babies play with new babysitters!

Every baby knows how to play *Scare the Babysitter*. The rules are simple:

☺   You can do anything you like, so long as it isn't dangerous.

☺   You aren't allowed to scare grandmas, but grandpas are fair game.

☺   You score points if the sitter gasps, screams or runs around in circles.

☺   You win if you get to five points, because babies get confused after they've run out of fingers on one hand (that's also why most baby rhymes only go up to five).

SuperBaby climbed out of his bouncy chair and turned it upside down. He went to the bookshelf and found a very big book. He threw it up in the air so that it landed with a huge thump. He screamed and wriggled back under his upturned chair.

Mad Mary came running downstairs.

Made her run! Baby point!

She gasped.

Another point! Now she'll say, "Oh no, poor baby!"

But Mad Mary put her hands on her hips and glared at him instead. 'Serves you right!' she said to the howling baby. 'I've a good mind to leave you there until you've learned your lesson!'

Lose a point! Bother!

Mad Mary flipped the chair the right way up and stuck the baby in it. She commanded, 'No kicking! No wriggling! Just sit still! If you fall over again, I'll *tie* you in!'

She went back upstairs. SuperBaby got out of the chair again, turned it over, found the book and threw it high in the air once more. When it landed he screamed; then he hid behind a big armchair.

Mad Mary was really mad this time. She ran downstairs, yanked the chair upright and snapped, 'I told you not to - '

She was speechless for a moment. This was a babysitter's nightmare: she had lost the baby.

Another point!

She started calling for him, sweetly at first. 'Baby... baby where are you? Come to lovely Mary. Come for a biggg hugggg... Baby?'

She searched the room while SuperBaby darted from one hiding place to another. This was fun!

'Baby! Come here, you stupid baby!'

Several worried minutes later, she caught up with him in the kitchen. He put on a guilty look and let her see his puffed-out cheeks.

'What have you got in your mouth?' she demanded. 'Spit it out!'

SuperBaby shook his head and puffed out his cheeks even more.

'What are you eating? Grapes? Marbles? Brussels sprouts?' – *Gasp* – 'Something you found in the cupboard? Oh no!'

He had three points now!

Mad Mary grabbed his face and tried to pry his jaws open. He kept them firmly clenched, so she squeezed his cheeks hard.

His mouthful of milk squirted out all over her.

'Yuk! You've splatted me with – what is that?

Milk?' She reached around behind him and grabbed the baby bottle he was hiding. 'How did you get the baby bottle out of the fridge?'

SuperBaby looked innocent. Mad Mary looked totally confused.

He was up to four points! He'd almost won!

She looked around at the fridge, which was firmly shut. When she looked back at SuperBaby again, his mouth was full once more.

'Spit it out!'

She got half-chewed grapes this time, all over her shoes. She shrieked and snatched him from the floor.

'Okay, baby: that was the last straw! You're going into your cot and you're staying there until you fall asleep. You don't mess with Mary!'

She carried the kicking, howling baby out of the kitchen.

Oh no! He would lose all his points if she put him to bed early! She would win!

SuperBaby wriggled in her arms as they passed through the living room. He grabbed at shelves, ornaments, lampshades, chair backs: anything to slow her down.

That made her *really* annoyed. She shifted her hold on him, juggling him about, trying to trap his arms. She gave him a little shake and then a little bounce into the air while she changed her grip.

Yes!!!!

In that tiny moment of freedom, SuperBaby shot up into the air and grabbed onto the fan blades above them in the middle of the living room. He scrambled on top of the blades. Fortunately, the fan wasn't on.

'What have I done?' Mad Mary gasped. 'I didn't mean to throw him that hard!'

All baby points back again!

She grabbed at his legs, but she wasn't tall enough to reach him.

'Bad baby!' she scolded. He put on his innocent look again and pretended to almost fall.

'No! Don't do that! *No no no no!*'

She dragged cushions off the armchairs and sofa and threw them on the floor for him to fall onto. It wasn't enough. He might break a leg or an arm or his cute baby neck! She looked around in a panic. The kitchen door was open and she could see…

She dashed into the kitchen and grabbed two loaves of bread and a big packet of marshmallows. She threw them on top of the cushions.

More! She needed more! Something soft and squashy! She found a package of tomatoes. A bag of mushrooms. Boxes of cereal. Grapes. Cupcakes. Three lettuces. Still not enough!

She ran upstairs and returned with armfuls of pillows. Now the floor was covered with soft things. But she still had to get the baby down. She found a broom in the kitchen and tried to knock him off the light fitting with it. He just laughed and pushed the broom away each time.

She said sweetly, 'I'll give you something nice if you come down. Want some sweeties? Or chocolates?' She ran into the kitchen again and came back with handfuls of tasty things. 'Crisps? Boiled eggs? Here, have an ice cream!'

SuperBaby stretched down an arm and took the ice cream. She snatched at him – but he was ready for that and she missed. He sat on the light fitting and ate the ice cream, not worrying about the bits that dribbled onto the light, the pillows, the boxes of cereal, the carpet, and onto Mad Mary's head…

She ran off again and came back with a stool. She placed this under the baby and climbed up on it.… The stool was a bit wobbly and she fell off onto the tomatoes, squashing them into the pillows. SuperBaby laughed.

She was furious now. 'Oh, you think it's funny, do you? *I'll* show you funny!'

She began throwing things at him. Tomatoes splatted on the ceiling. Mushrooms got caught in the light fitting. SuperBaby dodged cupcakes and marshmallows and grapes.

She got the vacuum cleaner out and tried to suck him down. She found a bit of rope and tried to lasso him. She ran out to the garden shed and dragged in a stepladder. She climbed it and snatched at him.

'Now I've got you! Ha ha!'

SuperBaby scooted to the far side of the light fixture and made faces at her. She made faces back.

'You're going to be in such trouble!' she warned. 'I'll tell your parents! I'll –'

There was a noise outside the front door. Mad

Mary froze. SuperBaby scampered to the end of the light fixture and dropped onto a cushion.

A key was turned in the lock.

Mad Mary slid down the stepladder and tried to hide it under the pillows and loaves of bread. SuperBaby crawled into a corner and began eating marshmallows from a bag.

They heard the front door opening. Then there were footsteps in the hallway and quiet voices warning each other not to wake the baby.

And now there were surprised faces at the living room door looking in at Mad Mary, who had ice cream in her hair, grapes and tomatoes squashed on her shirt, and bits of mushroom and crisps and boiled eggs sprinkled all over her.

'Oh – hello,' she said. A marshmallow dropped from the ceiling and landed on her nose.

SuperBaby's parents looked at her, at the spatters on the ceiling, at the soft and squashy things on the floor… and at SuperBaby, who had eaten all the marshmallows and now had his head stuck inside a cereal box.

'We were playing a game,' said Mad Mary.

'Oh, good,' said SuperBaby's mother. 'He likes games. You can babysit again!'

Dear Baby's Real Dairy

Mad Mary is coming to babysit again tomorrow. I've thought of some even better games to play with her. I hope she likes them!

The Mystery of Grandma's Knickers

Dear Dairy

I love mysteries. I always borrow mystery stories from the top bookshelf in the front room. That's where Mummy and Daddy keep the children's books they liked when they were at school. They think I might read them when I'm older, ha ha! My parents think I'm just looking at the pictures. Mummy thinks that Daddy takes the books down for me. Daddy thinks that Grandma does it. Grandma says she *knows* that Daddy is giving me Unsuitable Things to Play With.

Just now, SuperBaby wanted a new book to read. Maybe another Sherlock Holmes mystery! Usually he would fly up and get one, but Grandma was knitting in a corner of the room and she might notice a flying baby. So he poked Cat the Cat, who was curled up by SuperBaby's feet, dozing. She opened one eye.

'I need a book!' he whispered. He pointed at the

bookshelf above him.

She closed her eye again.

He promised, 'I'll get some of those fishy things out of the tin for you later!'

Cat the Cat opened both eyes. 'It's a deal,' she purred. Then she stretched, stood up, crept quietly behind the television, climbed onto a mantelpiece, stepped over a wooden duck and a pottery owl, and then leaped onto the bookshelf.

She walked along the top until she came to the place SuperBaby was pointing at. Then she leaned over, pawed delicately at a book and pushed it out slowly until it fell to the floor near SuperBaby's feet.

SuperBaby cried. Grandma looked up from her knitting. 'Did you drop your toy?' she asked kindly. 'Oh – your book. I don't know why your father lets you play with those, you'll just tear the pages. But here you are.'

SuperBaby smiled and opened the book. He sighed. *Mysteries were so good!* If only he had a real mystery to solve. But he didn't. *Maybe he never would…* That was such a sad thought that he started to cry and Grandma had to give him a big hug.

And later that day, Grandma gave him something even better: a *real* mystery....

When you're a baby, adults say things in your hearing that they would never say in front of a toddler. It's as if you're a piece of furniture or simply not there!

(You learned a lot of secrets when you were a baby, but you forgot them all. Or did you? Maybe they're still in your head somewhere. Maybe that explains why last year, at Great-Uncle Malcolm's funeral, you suddenly shouted out in Church, "He didn't fight in the war! He lost his foot dancing on a table in Thailand!")

SuperBaby always kept his ears open for Important Secrets and he was excited when Grandma said to his mother, over a cup of tea:

'Someone stole my knickers from the washing line in the back garden!'

'Which ones?' his mother asked.

'The big pink ones with the tiny flowers around the waist band. It's really odd, because those are quite an old pair. I had several nice new panties on the line too – expensive ones – but the thief only took the old pink ones!'

His mother exclaimed, 'How odd! Maybe they were just blown off by the wind?'

Grandma said in an offended tone, 'I peg all my clothes properly. They couldn't be blown off. And besides, the clothes peg was taken too!'

'Weird!'

'*It's a total mystery!*' concluded Grandma. And she would have been surprised to know why SuperBaby clapped his hands suddenly.

Half an hour later, when Grandma was putting on her coat to go home, SuperBaby held out his little arms for her and was given another big cuddle. He cried and cried when she tried to put him down, until finally she said to his mother exactly what SuperBaby had planned:

'Shall I take him to my house for the afternoon?'

'Yes, please! That would be lovely!' said SuperBaby's mother, rather too eagerly.

SuperBaby was *not* pleased that his mother clearly wanted to get rid of him for the afternoon, but he decided he would forgive her - just this once.

And so SuperBaby embarked on his very own mystery…

'First things first!' said Grandma once she'd pushed his pushchair around the corner to her little house. 'Let's wash those dirty hands! I don't want sticky baby fingers touching my special things!'

'No! MY first things first!' thought SuperBaby. 'Let's have a look at that washing line!'

So he pointed towards the wooden garden gate on the left of the house, which led into the garden.

'Oh? You'd like to play in the garden first? I suppose we could do that *before* washing your hands.'

Exactly! thought SuperBaby.

She took him into the house and then straight out the kitchen's back door into the garden. As the door clicked shut behind them, SuperBaby put on his Baby Detective face. He narrowed his eyes and tried to look wise.

'Oh dear,' said Grandma. 'Have you got a tummy ache? Let me burp you.'

No! I'm being a great Detective! This is how they look!

She put him over her shoulder and patted his back gently as she walked about the garden. It was rather embarrassing for a Great Detective to be burped while doing his work, but it was actually quite helpful: from up here he could see a lot more. He studied the grass, the flower beds, the shrubs and the two small trees (apple and plum). He peered at the fences. They were two metres high – but someone could climb that.

And the gate – surely they could have come in through the gate! Except that Grandma kept the gate locked. That was why she took him through the kitchen to get here.

There were some big trees beyond the far end of the garden, one of which had branches that dangled over the fence. A pitch-black crow, with feathers that stuck out untidily all over, was sitting on one of the branches and studying them.

'Caw!' said the crow, then dropped from the branch onto the grass, where it pecked at some bread Grandma had put out.

As SuperBaby watched the crow, he noticed something that set his detective heart racing: there was a clothes peg lying on the ground beneath that branch.

Yes! It was a clue! His first ever detective clue! The thief could have climbed that tree, crawled along a branch, and dropped into the garden like the crow just did. Then he would snatch the knickers and run back to the branch, dropping the clothes peg as he climbed back over!

That *must* be what had happened!

SuperBaby knew what he had to do: he had to find out what was on the other side of that fence. Maybe the Knicker Thief had a special Knicker House made completely out of old ladies' knickers!

'Caw!' said the crow, puzzling at SuperBaby with its little head tilted to one side. It shook its scruffy head at SuperBaby and flew away.

As Grandma was walking back along the garden to the house, they passed the washing line stretched between two wooden posts. SuperBaby pointed at the ground beneath it and made cute baby sounds.

'You want to sit on the grass?' She put him down and pulled up a light garden chair for herself.

SuperBaby crawled about beneath the clothes line, seeking more clues. Grass. Daisies. A tiny scrap of white paper. A piece of broken wooden clothes peg. Spatters of bird poo. A tiny screw.

'Caw!'

Well, that explained the bird poo: the crow had re-turned and was now balanced on the washing line above him.

'Go away!' Grandma scolded the crow. She felt in her apron pocket and threw a broken clothes peg at the bird, which missed. That explained the piece of peg SuperBaby had found…

'Arrrrk!' croaked the bird, pretending to have been hit. It swayed on the clothes line, then spun around on the wire and hung upside down.

'Caw!' it added. It shud-dered, gurgled, coughed horribly, and fell to the ground. It lay there in an untidy heap, groaning in a dying birdy manner.

'Oh no!' exclaimed Grandma. 'I didn't mean to hurt it! Poor bird!' She pushed herself up from her seat and hurried over to the crow.

'Arrrrrrrrkkkk…' it moaned. But the eye that was pointed towards SuperBaby appeared to wink.

Grandma said anxiously, 'I'd better get it something to eat. Oh dear – what can I give it? What do crows eat? I don't have any worms… I'll have to dig some up!'

She ran to the back of the house, where a garden fork and spade were leaning against the wall. She poked around with this in a flower bed for a few moments, then called out, 'I've got one! No – two!' before running back to the bird.

The crow had staggered to its feet and was swaying from side to side. It allowed Grandma to feed it a couple of worms, then some bird seed from the feeder, then three woodlice.

'I think that's enough,' said Grandma. 'We don't want to make it sick.'

The crow opened its beak wide, like a baby bird begging for its dinner.

Connie the crow! By Zoë Vickery

Grandma gave in. 'Well, maybe we should give it a little bread…'

Finally the bird seemed to have recovered. It flew up into the tree that overhung the back of the garden: the tree that the Pink Knicker Thief must have used to get into the garden. 'Caw!' it laughed.

And it definitely winked this time.

SuperBaby had a good time playing with Grandma, but his mind was elsewhere. He *had* to find out what was on the other side of the fence! He hoped Grandma might put him in his cot and have a little doze herself so he could fly off and investigate, but she kept busy until it was time to take him home.

He had to solve the mystery! He couldn't wait: the Pink Knicker Thief might strike again!

That night, he cried and pointed at his chest of drawers until his father brought out his black baby sleep suit for him to wear. Then SuperBaby pretended to fall asleep; but as soon as his door was shut, he called his friends for an emergency meeting.

'Grandma's pink knickers have been stolen!' he announced in a dramatic Detective voice.

'Nah,' said Rocky the Rat. 'She's probably just lost them. She's always losing things and forgetting things.'

SuperBaby said excitedly, 'I know why she does that! It's because of her hair!'

'What?'

SuperBaby said, 'I worked it out when I was practising being a Detective this week. I've been watching people, and I've noticed something: grey hair makes people lose things and forget things!'

'You're right,' agreed Cat the Cat. 'I've seen that! And grey hair makes them walk slow too.'

'*Squeak!*' said Mick the Mouse

'Mick says they oughta colour their hair,' said Rocky. 'Then they wouldn't have a problem.'

SuperBaby clapped his hands, exclaiming, 'We'll do that for Grandma! She'll be *so* pleased!'

Cat the Cat shook her head. 'Grandma won't let you mess with her hair. Lady humans are fussy about things like that.'

'Then we'll have to do it as a surprise,' said SuperBaby. 'Grandma won't mind that. She said she liked surprise presents when it was her birthday!'

After midnight, a baby flew unseen through the darkness. He was dressed in black and had darkened his face with chocolate spread. He carried a black shopping bag containing food colouring, a bicycle lamp, a half empty jar of chocolate spread, and three small quarrelling animals.

'Mick's trying to open the chocolate spread!' complained Cat the Cat from inside the bag.

'Cat the Cat keeps sitting on my tail!' said Rocky.

'Keep on your own side, then!' hissed the cat.

'Dis *is* my side!'

'Squeak!'

'Mick, leave dat alone.'

'Yes, leave it alone. That's not –'

'Awww, Mick!'

'Oh, yuk!'

'Squeak…'

'It's a bit late to be sorry now!'

'Be quiet now!' said SuperBaby. 'We've arrived!' He reached into the pocket of his sleep suit and took out the spare copy of Grandma's back door key he had borrowed from the kitchen shelf at home, along with the chocolate spread.

They crept through Grandma's back door, which opened into her little kitchen. He put the bag on the table there and peered inside it.

'All okay?' he asked.

'Ask *Mick* whether we're okay,' mewed an annoyed Cat the Cat.

'Yeah: Is we okay, Mick?' grumbled Rocky.

'*Squeak…*'

'Mick's got an apology to make. Go on, Mick.'

'*Squeak squeak squeakity squeak…*'

'Dat means he's sorry, 'cause he opened the wrong container. It wasn't chocolate spread he bit into.'

SuperBaby turned on the bicycle light and shone it inside the shopping bag. There were three rather pink animals inside.

'Oh no!' he said. 'Did all the pink dye spill out?'

'Dere's half left.'

'And we still have some other colours.'

SuperBaby said, 'But pink is Grandma's favourite colour!'

'*Squeak!*'

'Mick says his favourite colour is blue.'

They crept into Grandma's bedroom, as quiet as mice – well actually, as quiet as a mouse, a cat, a rat and a flying baby. She was fast asleep.

They coloured as much of her hair as they could

reach. They got quite a lot on the pillow, but that was because she wouldn't keep her head still.

'Dis would be easier with your dad,' whispered Rocky the Rat. 'Men don't mind having their hair messed about. Mick could make a nest in your dad's hair and he wouldn't notice.'

'I bet he *would* notice!' whispered SuperBaby.

'Wouldn't,' said Rocky.

'Wouldn't,' agreed Cat the Cat.

'Would!' insisted SuperBaby.

'*Squeak!*'

'Mick says dere's only one way to find out…'

And then Mick squeaked so loud that the others had to shush him.

'Dere's no owls here, Mick.'

'*Squeak!*'

Everyone looked to the shelf by the bed, where his tiny mouse finger was pointing; and then they all laughed.

'Those aren't real,' said Cat the Cat. 'Grandma has little pottery owls all over the house.'

'*Squeak!*'

'He don't like the way they're lookin' at him.'

'*Squeak.*'

'You're daft, Mick. You're daft as a pink mouse. But yeah, let's stop 'em from starin' at us.'

Mick and Rocky took something from the bag and carried it up onto the shelf: the jar of chocolate spread. They dealt with the owls while the others continued to cure Grandma's grey hair problem.

When their work was finished, SuperBaby and his friends tiptoed away. They locked Grandma's kitchen door behind them and SuperBaby led them to the end of the back garden.

'See?' said SuperBaby. 'Look at that branch over-head, and the clothes peg on the grass beneath it. That's what detectives call a Clue.'

Cat the Cat said, 'It looks like an ordinary clothes

peg to me. And an ordinary branch.'

'*Squeak.*'

'Nah,' said Rocky. 'Dere ain't no owls here, Mick. Dat bird up dere lookin' at us as if we're stark ravin' mad is a crow. And it's probably right.'

SuperBaby said, 'The owls could be hiding. I hope there *are* some. I like owls!'

Rocky laughed. 'You wouldn't like 'em if you was a mouse. By the way, why are we standin' here in the middle of the night lookin' at a branch?'

SuperBaby explained, 'It's the branch that the Pink Knicker Thief uses when he climbs into the garden. We must investigate it! We have to follow his trail into the other garden!'

Cat the Cat shrugged her shoulders, then leapt elegantly onto the branch. SuperBaby flew after her.

Rocky and Mick looked at each other.

'Squeak?'

'Yeah, totally agree, Mick. Let's go the easy route. Old school.' And the two rodents scampered under the fence instead.

It was dark on the branch and it grew even darker as SuperBaby and the cat crept along the branch into the blackness of the tree, before dropping to the ground on the other side.

'Quiet now!' whispered SuperBaby as his friends gathered about him. 'The Pink Knicker Thief probably has an armed guard and listening devices and booby traps and other scary things!'

They crept around this new garden for ten minutes... then circled the house for ten minutes... then looked in through the windows.

There was a little girl living in the house who had been sad for two years. In all that time, she had never smiled or laughed. Her parents were very worried about this and had taken her to many doctors and therapists who asked her questions, told her happy things, read comics to her, showed her cartoons and even stood on their heads for her. But nothing worked.

She woke now and heard whispers at the window near her bed, and tiny scritchings and scrabblings on the window ledge. She cautiously drew back her curtain and looked out the open window....

The starlight illuminated three rather pink furry animals sitting on her window ledge, plus a baby with a lot of chocolate spread plastered about his face.

'Ooops!' said the baby. 'We were looking for the Pink Knicker Thief. Wrong house. Sorry!' Then he tucked the pink cat and the two pink rodents into a black shopping bag and flew away.

The little girl laughed for hours.

Pink Knicker Thievery Continued

SuperBaby was very tired from his night time adventures and slept late the next morning. He awoke to a fuzzy memory of something foolish that he and his friends had done after getting back from Grandma's house.

What was it? He pulled the chocolate spread jar from under his pillow, opened the lid and had a little lick as he tried to remember. It was something to do with … with …

His father put his head around the door and said cheerily, 'Good morning!'

SuperBaby quickly hid the chocolate spread under his covers and made the appropriate baby noises.

His father turned his head and called along the hallway, 'Baby's awake!' As he did this, SuperBaby saw something unusual in his father's hair. Then he remembered: They had dared Mick the Mouse to try something...

Mick the Mouse was waving at SuperBaby from the nest he'd made in his father's scruffy, fluffy light brown hair. Well, *most* of it was brown. It had some green and blue patches too now (they'd used all the pink at Grandma's).

'Oh no! Mick!' exclaimed SuperBaby in horror.

His father put his head back in the room. 'What did you say?'

'Ba ba oh no bo gick!' said SuperBaby. But he was thinking: *I hope you don't see Mick and put him into one of those nasty mousetraps!*

SuperBaby tried to signal to Mick to jump off, but his father had already walked away to the bathroom. *Oh no! He would wash his face... he would look in the mirror... and it would be Bye bye, Mick!*

SuperBaby started to cry. 'I've lost my friend forever!' he sobbed.

His mother came into the room with a telephone in her hand. She picked up SuperBaby, put him on the mat and began changing his nappy with one hand while talking to someone.

'Pink?!!' she was saying. 'And green and a bit of blue?!! But how?'

It was Grandma on the phone! She must be so happy about her new hair! Of course, the first thing she would do is phone and tell everyone!

SuperBaby's mother listened, wiped, slipped a new nappy under SuperBaby's bottom and said, 'Well, I don't see how the police could help, Mum.'

Then she exclaimed, 'Chocolate spread? On your pottery owls?'

Oops. Mick and Rocky had hidden the staring eyes of the owls by covering their little faces with chocolate spread... then licked it off... covered the faces again... licked it off again... and so on.

SuperBaby's mother carried SuperBaby back to his cot, still talking on the phone. 'Did you leave the door unlocked? Maybe it was one of those kids from next door – Wait a moment – *What's this?*'

Something was poking out from the end of SuperBaby's cot blanket. Something that looked like a chocolate spread jar.

She said to Grandma, 'I'll phone you later. My husband is in *so* much trouble just now!'

'Why?' asked a voice from the doorway.

SuperBaby's mother lifted a nearly empty jar of chocolate spread from the bed. 'So that's where you hid it!' she said. 'That's why it wasn't in the pantry this morning!'

'I didn't –'

'And you took it to my mother's house and spread it on her owls!'

'I didn't –'

'And look at your hair! What have you done to it? Is that hair dye?'

'I didn't –'

'You've dyed it green and blue! And you dyed my mother's hair, too! It *must* have been you! And the cat's half pink as well!'

'I didn't –'

'And what's… that… *in* your hair? It's – (*shriek*) – a mouse! A pink mouse!'

'What?'

Mick the Mouse did a little victory dance before leaping onto the wardrobe - and then onto the cot railing – and then scampered to the end of the cot – and then threw himself onto the window sill and squeezed out the window.

'It wasn't me!' SuperBaby's father insisted.

'Well, it wasn't the baby, was it?'

SuperBaby was sorry that his father was in trouble again: but actually his father didn't seem to mind.

His father was a quiet, well-behaved man. He had a dull job as an accountant, and he liked the idea that he was now a notorious and reckless swashbuckler who dyed the hair of old ladies in their sleep and plastered chocolate spread on their owls.

SuperBaby spent the morning thinking about all his clues. They were very confusing, which made the mystery of the pink knickers even more mysterious. He *had* to go back to Grandma's and find out more!

So he whined and grumbled until his mother got the hint and took him for a stroll in his pushchair, stopping at Grandma's for a cup of tea. He pretended to fall asleep in Grandma's arms, knowing that his mother would let Grandma look after him for an hour or so until he woke.

It was Grandma's nap time and he knew what she would do: she would put him back in his pushchair and then doze off herself in her big armchair. He waited until she was snoring softly, then unfastened himself.

He flew out through the big glass doors – *bonk!* *Ouch!* He stopped and opened them first. *Then* he flew out.

He zoomed around the little garden, zigzagging across it, studying the grass and fence line at high speed. There *had* to be more clues! But he didn't see any... *Bother!*

He landed in the overhanging tree branches and studied the garden from this angle.

'There *must* be at least *one* clue!' he insisted.

'Why?' asked a voice behind him.

SuperBaby turned around. That black, scruffy crow was perched on a branch behind him. Its little head was tilted to one side and it was studying the baby with a beady black eye.

SuperBaby said, 'Because it's a mystery. All mysteries have clues. You just have to know where to look for them.'

'What's the mystery then?' the crow asked.

'Grandma's pink knickers have been knicker-napped!'

The crow poked a feather into place with its bill. 'Nah. Ain't a mystery. *I* took 'em.'

SuperBaby gasped. 'You?'

'Yep. Don't look so surprised. We crows aren't totally incapable of a knicker heist. We've got the right tools, see?'

The crow held up one set of claws. 'Opposable digits,' it said proudly.

'What?'

'My back claw is opposite my front three. See? That means I can pick up things with my feet. Most animals can't. *You* can't, for instance.'

'I can use my hands, though!' said SuperBaby.

'You're lucky. Most animals don't have hands. As for me, I've got no hands, but I can tie a bow with my beak and feet instead. You just ask a cat to do that. The cat will turn into a nervous wreck after trying for a few minutes.'

The crow tilted its head back and gave a triumphant *caw*. 'Ha! It always gets 'em. They're about to leap upon you: but you challenge 'em to a Shoelace Tying Duel, and they just go to pieces. *Caw!*'

SuperBaby was impressed. 'That's amazing!' he said. Then he remembered his manners. 'My name is SuperBaby and I look after my parents and grandparents. Who are you?'

'I'm Connie the Crow and I look after my friends and family - and I con everyone else.'

SuperBaby held out a hand and Connie held out a crow's foot. They shook hand to foot solemnly.

SuperBaby asked, 'What's a con?'

Connie winked at him. 'A con's a sneaky trick. We crows are good at that.'

'Is that why you take the knickers?' asked SuperBaby. 'Is it a trick you're playing?'

Connie flapped up nearer to the baby, bent her head close and whispered, 'Nah! It's because of the Spies!'

'What?'

'You know – the CIA and MI5 and KGB and FBI and SMERSH and all them lot. They're always trying to steal our crow secrets.'

'But how do pink knickers – '

'Shhh! Not so loud. They've got microphones and microwaves and wireless thingies *everywhere!*'

'Sorry,' whispered SuperBaby. 'How do the pink knickers help?'

'Pink knickers have a special electromagnetic property that causes them to scramble signals.'

'You mean smoke signals? Like Red Indians make? I read about those in one of Daddy's old books.'

'Nah. These are Radio Wave signals the spies send to satellites. Special infrared ultraviolet thingies.'

'How do the knickers stop the signals?'

Connie the Crow shrugged her birdy black shoulders. 'Search me. I expect it's the combination of the pink light spectrum with the electrostatic properties of the knicker elastic.'

'That sounds very scientific,' said SuperBaby. 'And like most science I've read so far, it doesn't make much sense.'

Connie the Crow winked at him. 'Or I could just be making this up.' She fell off the branch and rolled about laughing on the grass.

'Oh. *Are* you making it up?'

Connie sat up. 'Yep. The real reason is much scarier. I didn't want to tell you in case you started howling and gave away the secret.'

SuperBaby put on a Brave Detective face. 'I'm not scared of anything!' he promised.

'All right… but stop me if you can't take any more. You see, there's some aliens that are trying to take over the world, starting with the crows. They send down tiny evil robots that inject alien brain cells into our eggs. So when the baby crows are born, they're really aliens. And then the alien crows fly to the cots of little babies and… Are you sure you want to hear this bit?'

'Yes!'

'Well, those evil alien crows peck holes into the babies' heads and put alien brain cells inside *them*. And so the babies turn into aliens too. It's horrible!'

'Oh no!' gasped SuperBaby. 'So those babies at the Mother and Baby Group that Mummy takes me to… Are they… *aliens*? That would explain a lot.'

'Only the ones with curly blond hair. That's how you can tell. And later on, they grow up to be brainless celebrities on reality TV.'

'So how can they be stopped?' asked SuperBaby.

Connie bent her head close and whispered, 'Maybe you can help us! Let me show you what we do with the knickers.'

She flew off and SuperBaby flew after her to the top branches of the tree, where an untidy crow's nest was balanced in a crook of branches.

Crows' nests always look as if the crow had randomly dropped sticks from a great height and some of them just happened to get caught in the branches. But this nest looked as if the crow had its eyes shut when it dropped the sticks …. and then stretched a large pair of pink knickers over and around the chaotic pile of sticks.

'See this?' asked the crow, landing on her untidy nest and pecking at the knickers. 'Holds it all together, right? And it gets rid of aliens at the same time.'

'How?'

'The pinkness makes their robot eyes go funny. They get dizzy and fall over, and their tiny robot legs get stuck in the special scratchy knicker fabric they use for old ladies. And then the static electricity in the knickers zaps the robot's electrical circuits.'

SuperBaby flew around the crow's nest, making the same polite approving noises he'd heard his mother make when being shown around someone else's house.

The crow continued, 'And look at the other nests round about: we've done the same to them all. We've got an alien-free zone here. A kind of crow neighbourhood watch, know what I mean?'

SuperBaby looked around. All the crows' nests in sight had a flash of pink about them.

'Is this the only thing you need to fight the aliens?' he asked.

'Yeah. Works a treat. Just wish we had more of 'em. Another pair here would make it totally alien proof in all weathers. And maybe we could expand the boundaries. Spread the word to the other crows in this town, then all over Hampshire... England... the World!'

'Wow!' said SuperBaby.

'Yeah,' said Connie the Crow with a big sigh. 'Just wish we could find someone to help us gather more pink knickers... The humans are onto us and they've got cats watchin' most of the washing lines. Yep, we need a Hero. *Sigh.'*

SuperBaby exclaimed, '*I* can do that!'

'Really? Aw, that would be great!'

So... Over the next week, SuperBaby used any chance he had to zoom around the neighbourhood, looking for large pink knickers flapping on washing lines. Most days he found at least one pair.

He always wore his father's sunglasses as he went knicker hunting, so that no one would know who he was. And when he found some knickers, he put them on his head as he flew home: he knew that would really confuse people!

He piled the knickers inside the cupboard behind

his bed, the one that was full of cuddly toys he never used. He kept the sunglasses on top of the pile, and sometimes he kept a jar of chocolate spread there too, just in case he needed some extra energy and a face disguise.

Soon he had twenty pairs of baggy pink knickers! Connie the Crow would be so pleased when she came to get them on Saturday!

But Saturday was his parents' cleaning day, and while SuperBaby was reading a scary crime novel on the floor of his room, his mother was dusting shelves… and window ledges… and cupboards….

She opened the cupboard before SuperBaby could stop her. She picked up the jar of chocolate spread.

'What?' she asked.

Then she picked up the sunglasses that belonged to SuperBaby's father.

'What??!!' she repeated.

She counted the pairs of large pink knickers.

'WHAT???!!!' she exclaimed. 'Oh, that man!'

She threw everything back into the cupboard and ran downstairs, shouting for SuperBaby's father.

Uh-oh!

SuperBaby flew to the cupboard, grabbed the knickers and flew them out the window. He stuck them upside down over the chimney pot and flew back into his room.

He heard his parents' footsteps coming up the stairs. His mother didn't sound happy! He tucked the chocolate spread under his pillow and sat on the floor again.

She was at the door! *Oh no - he was still holding the sunglasses in his hand!*

When his mother stormed in, he was "pretending"

to read his book again, wearing Daddy's sunglasses.

His mother marched his father to the cupboard and pointed inside. 'Look at that pile of knickers!' she said angrily. 'What kind of joke are you playing now? Are you the Pink Knicker Thief that's been stealing knickers from all over the neighbourhood?'

'Uh... Where?' asked SuperBaby's father.

'There! Under the jar of chocolate spread *you* keep taking from the kitchen, and under *your* sunglasses!'

'Are they... are they *invisible* pink knickers? And are those other things invisible as well?'

She pushed him aside and looked in. She moved the toys around, then pulled them all out onto the floor and stuck her head deep into the cupboard.

She insisted, 'They were right there on the shelf. I *saw* them!'

SuperBaby tried not to laugh as his parents stared inside the empty cupboard.

'You must have imagined it,' said SuperBaby's father to the puzzled mother as they replaced the cuddly toys.

'I didn't! Someone must have moved them!'

SuperBaby's father smiled. At last! It was *his* turn

to say it! 'Well, it wasn't the baby, was it?'

.... Later that morning, Connie the Crow landed on the window ledge and peered in at SuperBaby, who was bouncing in his cot and doing back flips.

'Caw!' she called and tapped on the window with her beak. SuperBaby checked outside his door to make sure his parents were busy downstairs before flying to the window and opening it.

'I hung the knickers on the chimney!' he said to the crow.

She nodded. 'Yeah, I saw that. Thanks. But I thought that, since you've been so good to me and all that, maybe I oughta tell you the real reason why I wanted them baggy pink knickers.'

'Oh,' said SuperBaby. 'It wasn't the robot aliens?'

'Nah. I made that up.'

'So it really was because of the spies?'

'Nah. I made that up too.'

'Was it something even more amazing?'

'Nah. We just use the knickers to hold our nests together. It stops our eggs and baby chicks from fallin' out between the sticks. We ain't much good at nest buildin', innit?'

SuperBaby thought about this. It seemed to make much more sense than the other reasons Connie had told him.

Connie said gently, 'If you're gonna learn to be a great detective, you've gotta ask me some proper detective questions now.'

SuperBaby nodded and said, 'In the mystery books, they call that *testing the evidence!*' He thought really hard this time before asking, 'Why do you choose old lady knickers?'

Connie said, 'You gotta have big baggy panties so they stretch around the whole nest. Them fancy little knickers what covers nuffink much ain't no use to us at all.'

'And why only the pink ones?'

Connie seemed embarrassed. 'It's just the fashion, innit? Last year, it was black. This year, you gotta have pink ones or the other crows all laugh at you.'

'Oh… I'm not a very good detective, am I?' SuperBaby asked sadly.

'Nah - not yet. But you're a very nice baby and you've got a crow what's your friend forever, if you'd like that.'

'That's better that being a good detective! It's even better than being a *great* detective!' SuperBaby exclaimed.

'Caw!' replied Connie and flew off to collect the stash of knickers.

Baby Steps and Baby Love

Dear Dairy

I'm only six months old, so I'm not planning to say my first words for a while. I'm going to wait for my first birthday party. AND I'm not going to let the adults know I can understand what they say because they'll start bossing me about!

I AM planning on walking soon. Why? NUMBER 1 (I have learned about Numbers and they are fun). It will make Mummy happy. She keeps reading books about what babies are expected to do at my age. Then she looks at me sadly and sighs. So I will walk before she does the Sad Look about that. NUMBER 2 I'M FED UP WITH CRAWLING AROUND! It hurts my knees and I hate being down on the floor.

You probably think the floor is clean. But imagine you're a baby with your nose just above the floor half the time ... and your hands are rubbing the dirty places that shoes and feet have walked on ... and you're breathing the dust and hair and dandruff and scurfy bits from the skin of everyone who visits.

You touch all the coffee stains and cookie crumbs and woodlice and dead flies, and the dried dog slobber from Aunt Sissy's visit with her four hair-dropping, drooling, widdling doggies.

Yuk!

SuperBaby planned to walk *perfectly* from the first step. He didn't want to stagger around like the toddlers he saw at the mother and baby group. So he spent hours practising at night.

He didn't enjoy walking. Flying was so much easier! And it was so exciting! Walking was *boring*.

Walking about in his cot at night was so boring that he decided to mix it up a bit. So he jumped around in his cot instead.

Ouch!

He hit the Planets of the Solar System mobile above his bed. He had Jupiter tangled in his hair and Mercury trying to become an earring.

He needed more light! He flew to the window and opened the curtains. The lamp post from the street lit up the room now. That was better!

The people across the road were watching him with binoculars again: he could see the light reflecting off the lenses. He waved at them and flew back to his cot. He did some more high bounces, waving each time. Ouch! He hit his head on the ceiling!

He jumped once more in the air and did a somersault, landing on the carpet. He walked about gracefully like the queen on TV, then he slouched around like Granddad. But walking was still boring!

So he turned upside down and walked on his hands instead. He walked on his hands across the room… up the wall… onto the window ledge… and he waved at the people across the road with his foot this time. They seemed to be getting a camera out, so he dropped to the floor again and walked about on his hands some more.

His mother opened the door and peeked inside. A shaft of light from outside highlighted SuperBaby walking about on his hands. She gasped and turned her head to shout to SuperBaby's father:

'The baby's – he's - upside down! Come quick!'

There were feet running along the hallway, then

the door was pushed all the way open and the light was turned on.

SuperBaby *was* upside down – his feet were on his cot pillow and his head was at the bottom of his tiny quilt. He was making snuffling sounds like a baby sleeping, and not like a baby walking upside down.

His father said, 'That's sweet. I thought something must be wrong.'

His mother said, 'But he was walking on his hands! On the carpet!'

'Okay… I think you need a cup of cocoa…'

The next night, SuperBaby was just about to bounce out of bed again when he heard a gentle sound from outside his door. He dropped down in his cot and peered through its bars as the door opened slowly and quietly. A face peeked in, then withdrew. The door was left open a crack as SuperBaby's mother walked away.

Bother!

No walking practice for a while. He would have to find something else to do. He felt under his pillow and took out the needle and black cotton thread hidden there.

An hour later, his mother peeked in again. All was quiet and she came in to straighten the sleeping baby's cover. She stopped, peered more closely and exclaimed under her breath:

'Not again! Oh, that man!'

She ran out and returned a few minutes later, dragging SuperBaby's father by the arm. 'This is *not* funny!' she whispered. 'I put him to bed in his brand new sleep suit – and look at that!'

'I'm… looking… but… what am I seeing?'

'Don't pretend you don't know!'

'I'm not pretending… but… umm… What is it I don't know?'

'There! On the sleep suit!'

'Awww. That's so sweet. You bought him a sleep suit with an "S" on it. "S" for – '

'No I didn't! *You* put it there! You mustn't draw on his sleep suits! I keep telling you – the ink washes out and stains everything in the washing machine!'

'But I didn't – '

'Yes you did! Just look at that "S". You drew that – Oh. You didn't…. You sewed it on this time!'

'I can't sew. I'm useless at things like that.'

'Ha! You're telling me the baby did it?'

SuperBaby slept on, hearing none of this. He was dreaming about his name.

He shared his name with his favourite cartoon character. And sometimes in his dreams, he *was* the cartoon character. That's why he often laughed in his sleep.

SuperBaby hadn't liked his name to start with. Then one day his father let him sit on his lap and watch some old Looney Tunes cartoons. SuperBaby laughed so much he wet himself. He wet his father's leg, too: the cartoon was that funny.

He *loved* his name now. He loved it so much that he'd started drawing a big S on his sleep suits and on some of his shirts. It stood for SuperBaby and – well, I expect you'll work it out if I tell you he sometimes whispered, "Suffering succotash!" to himself.

When his mother started complaining about the ink stains, SuperBaby began sewing on the S instead. His mother thought his father was doing it, his father thought Grandma was doing it, and Grandma thought it was the Tooth Fairy. Or maybe it was Granddad: Grandma said that he Couldn't be Trusted to Behave.

But just now, SuperBaby had something else to worry about. Recently his parents had used a new word, "Holiday". He didn't understand what a Holiday was, but was a new thing, and new things always worried him.

He'd read stories in Grandma's magazines where people had Holiday Romances: but the stories didn't explain what holidays were, or why people had them.

He didn't understand the Romance part of the stories either, but it seemed to involve kissing and disappointment.

He asked his friends, who weren't helpful. Rocky and Mick had no idea. Ben the Box and Rick the Brick said nothing, as usual.

Cat the Cat shook her head gravely. 'Holidays are when people go away,' she said. 'Your parents will probably put you in a cage in a big building full of other babies in cages. That's what they did with me, when they went on holiday before you were born.'

'And that Romance thing don't ever work out,' said Connie the Crow. 'You end up with a nestful of chicks you gotta feed day and night. I expect a Holiday Romance means sittin' in a big cage feedin' worms and spiders to other babies.'

SuperBaby tried not to cry, but it was hard.

The next day was Friday. SuperBaby's mother took him to the shops in his pushchair, so he could try on some new baby shoes for the Holiday.

She closed the front gate behind her and waited to cross the road. The people from the house opposite were in their front garden, snipping twigs off rose bushes. They came to their own gate and watched as SuperBaby's mother pushed the buggy across the road. She waved at them.

The Man stroked his beard. The Woman snapped her rose cutters. They looked at SuperBaby.

'We know all about it,' said the Man.

'It shouldn't be allowed,' said the Woman.

'We're going to tell!' they both said.

'Pardon?' said SuperBaby's mother.

'One day,' said the man. 'One day we'll have evidence. And then – ah ha!' He snapped his cutters.

'You're not as clever as you think you are!' the woman said. 'Shed smasher!'

SuperBaby waved at them. *'Gaga googoo!'* he laughed, then blew a big baby raspberry over his shoulder as his puzzled mother wheeled him away.

His new shoes turned out to be something called "sandals" which felt silly, looked silly and tasted disgusting. *He knew he should stop putting things in his mouth, but he was a baby, so it felt normal to give everything a quick chew. Even shoes.*

The sandals made his feet feel cold and they let in nettles, stones and lost ants. SuperBaby decided they were invented by people who don't like feet.

On Saturday morning, his father put the new sandals on SuperBaby's feet. Then his mother took them off and put them on the correct way around. His father carried SuperBaby to the car and strapped him into his baby seat. His mother loaded the car with bags full of things that made no sense to SuperBaby.

Why was there a tiny bucket and spade in one bag? Were they planning to plant him somewhere??!

He watched where they were driving and tried to memorise the turns, in case he had to escape from the Baby Cage and fly back home by himself. But as usual the car noise and movement made him very sleepy … and he couldn't keep his eyes open and…

… He woke to find that he was being lifted out of the car. They had come to a very strange place.

There was an odd roaring noise in the distance, like an enormous monster grumbling and snarling to itself. It sounded a bit bubbly and gurgly too, as if it was foaming at the mouth while it swallowed things.

He could hear a lot of children laughing, squealing… and sometimes *screaming*. Maybe they were being put into cages! Or fed to the monster!

And as they walked away from the car, he wondered if he was having a bad dream, because so much was clearly wrong.

The air had a sharp, salty smell. There was maybe a tiny scent of fish in it. The birds were white and had shrill, sharp voices. The ground was the wrong colour too: it was a grimy shade of white and didn't have much grass in it.

He looked down and found that there were monsters that lived in small holes in the ground. One of them popped out of a hole and waved a long, shell-like claw at him. Its eyes were on stalks and it had lots of scary jointed legs. Maybe it was a baby version of the Sea Monster!

Then he looked forward and saw the Monster itself: its big blue-green-grey watery mouth was opened wide, stretching left and right and far into the distance, with loose, wrinkled lips flecked with foam. It roared and bubbled and slobbered at him.

It had already gobbled up a few children and their parents! SuperBaby could see their heads bobbing about on its slippery tongue. Some tried to scramble back to the beach, but the spit in the monster's mouth swelled and bubbled about them hungrily, dragging its shrieking victims back into its gullet.

This was worse than the Baby Cage! SuperBaby began to struggle and cry, pointing back to the car.

His parents laughed at him. 'He's afraid of the Sea! How funny!'

It's not *funny!* SuperBaby thought. *There's a big Sea Monster out there gobbling up children, and you don't care! Don't you see it??*

They wouldn't let go of him. They continued to take him closer to the Sea Monster.

SuperBaby had read about monsters in the books his parents let him play with. He knew there were things like Krakens and Leviathans. He hadn't realised that they were so enormous. And he hadn't realised that parents took their little children to feed to the monster, like a sacrifice in the old tales.

SuperBaby cried louder and tried harder to escape. But his parents just held him tighter. They were getting annoyed with him now, too.

'Hush! People are looking at us!'

SuperBaby stopped crying. He resolved to fight the Sea Monster, and die bravely.

His parents made their way between half-naked people dozing in long chairs or lying about untidily on towels, with bits of their body hanging out everywhere. They went past children digging in the sand, and weaved in and out of lines of stringy green weeds until they found a patch where they could set down their blankets, bags, buckets and baby.

He was free!

SuperBaby's resolution to suffer death bravely evaporated as soon as his sandal-clad feet touched the warm sand. He sprang to his feet and ran away.

His parents watched, open-mouthed.

SuperBaby's first public steps were pretty amazing for a six month old baby. They would have been even more graceful if he wasn't wearing sandals that collected sand at every stride!

His other problem was that there were too many floppy body parts to avoid. He was looking back to see if the growling Sea Monster was chasing him when he ran straight into a large, flabby backside of someone bending over to take their shoes off. He bounced off and landed on the sand, right in what seemed to be lump of wet jelly. *Yuk!*

The jelly had little tentacles poking out, which stung him. Another sea beast!

He shot off in another direction, with his parents in pursuit. He stubbed a toe on a discarded plastic bucket and fell onto the chest of a lady who was reading a book while her children skipped off happily to be eaten by the Sea Monster. She shouted at him and he rolled away, but – *oh no!*

His fingers had become tangled in the cords of her swim suit top, and he somehow pulled it off – and then she shrieked - and then he panicked and threw the top in the air. It landed on his father's head and got snared in his sunglasses.

SuperBaby dodged left and right, knocked someone's ice cream into the air (caught it, gave it a lick, handed it back) and jumped over a crab that was dancing about while snapping its claws at him.

He was getting away! Hooray! He was going to be safe! But… Mummy and Daddy wouldn't be safe. The Sea Monster would eat them…

That sad thought made him slow down. Maybe he should lure his parents away before the Sea Monster could suck them in.

His mother snatched at him from one side, so he jumped away and ran faster. A big white bird screeched at him from above, and his father shouted at him from behind. He missed his footing, tripped, sailed through the air and…

… And there was the cutest little girl he had ever seen.

She had blond curls and a sweet smile. She had turned the smile towards him as he was dodging about. He was clearly the most amazing baby she had seen. He was super fit!

The cute smile wavered as SuperBaby tripped, sailed through the air and then landed smack on top of the lovely big sand castle that the little girl had been sculpting into perfection.

And now the smile was gone. Tears ran down her pretty face. She whacked SuperBaby on the backside with her plastic shovel.

This was embarrassing!

His parents snatched him up and apologised to the little girl's parents.

Her mother said, 'That's all right. Little Maria can always build another sand castle. Can't you, Maria?'

Maria considered this and nodded her head slowly. She wiped her face with sandy fingers and looked thoughtfully at SuperBaby.

'Aww, how cute!' said her mother. 'Give the naughty boy a kiss to show you're not mad with him, Maria.'

So SuperBaby got his first kiss when he was only six months old. And then Maria whacked him over the head with her plastic spade.

As he was being carried back towards the Sea Monster and his place on the beach, he watched the cute blond-haired girl carefully putting her wrecked sand castle back together.

He sighed. He had been puzzled when he read about Holiday Romance, but now he understood what it meant: you got one kiss and a sore head. And you never saw her again.

Or did you?

Supermarket Adventures

SuperBaby loved almost everything about the supermarket. It
had exciting smells and plenty of
odd things to look it. It also had
lots of people with interesting
looks on their faces. Some of
them looked flustered. Some
looked annoyed. A lot of them
just looked hungry, which is how
SuperBaby always felt in the supermarket.

One morning, he was sitting in his cot, dressed up
ready to go out on a supermarket journey.

'Why've you got funny clothes on?' asked Rocky
the Rat from the top of the wardrobe, where SuperBaby had made a guest room for him, using an
old shoebox.

SuperBaby said, 'Mummy's taking me to the shops.
We're going to buy lots of food and some scary stuff
like bleach. She has a list. She likes lists. I think all
Mummies do. They even make lists for Daddies, but

I think the Daddies lose them because Mummy is always saying things like "It's on the list I gave you." and then Daddy says, "What list?"'

'Humans are crazy,' said Rocky. 'Aren't they, Mick?' he asked Mick the Mouse, who was sitting next to him on the wardrobe.

'*Squeak!*' Mick agreed.

Cat the Cat was on the window ledge, cleaning around her ears with a paw. She said, 'Their thoughts keep falling out of their heads, so they have to write them down.'

'Yeah,' said Rocky. 'But you don't need a list for food. You just grab it and run, right?'

SuperBaby said, 'That wouldn't work in a supermarket because there's so much of everything in the shop. The food is stacked up *everywhere*! Nobody ever knows which things to get, so they have to take a list of what they want.'

Rocky the Rat was astonished at this behaviour. 'Wot?' he asked. 'Don't they just grab the first thing they come across and eat it right there in the shop?'

Cat the Cat began cleaning around her other ear before saying, 'Surely they chase the tasty things around the shop until they catch one of them, and then they play with it for a while. And when they get bored with that, they bite its head off.'

SuperBaby said, 'No! You put what you want into a big basket on wheels and you push the basket all the way around the shop and fill it right up to the top, and then you take it outside to the car park. It's a nice game called *shopping*. Mummies do it all the time and Daddies do it if you make them.'

Mick squeaked excitedly, for quite a long time.

Rocky said, 'He says then you throw everything into a big hole and run back inside and grab lots more stuff and throw that into another hole and run back inside and – well, you keep doing that until an owl or fox turns up and tries to kill you.'

'*Squeak!*'

'Or a cat.'

Cat the Cat pretended not to hear this.

SuperBaby said, 'You don't put shopping in a hole. You load it into the car and bring it home and put it into cupboards.'

'Same thing,' said Rocky. 'A cupboard is just a hole wiv a door on it, right?'

Cat the Cat asked, 'Are there any specially tasty things there? Meat? Birds? Fish? Mice?' She winked at Mick.

'There's lots of nice meaty things! And there's a special fish place which smells funny because it's got a lot of fish there, sleeping on beds of ice.'

Rocky asked, 'Nuts? Chocolate? Chips? Biscuits?'

'It's full of things like that too! Any food you can think of! And there's other things that no one really wants, like soap and glasses and shoes.'

'*Squeak?*' asked Mick.

Rocky shook his head. 'They won't have shoes for mice. What do you want shoes for anyway?'

'*Squeak!*'

'Don't be daft. Mice don't play football.'

'*Squeak.*'

'They still wouldn't play if they had shoes.'

'*Squeak.*'

'No they wouldn't.'

Cat the Cat's eyes were gleaming as she asked, 'Can

anyone go the shop and take what they want? Cats, for instance?'

'Or rats?'

'Squeak?'

SuperBaby thought about this. 'There are big machines that look at your shopping and make beeping noises. Maybe the machines would stop you.'

'Squeak!'

'Yeah, Mick: scary machines like big metal owls.'

Cat the Cat gave a disappointed *mew*. 'I don't like being beeped at. Maybe you could just nab a big fish for me and bring it home.'

Rocky asked, 'Can I come along? Just to see?'

'Squeak?'

'You can both come! But you'll have to hide.'

Then SuperBaby flew onto the chest of drawers where his mother had left her phone. He opened the list on her phone and added some items she had forgotten: sardines and tuna (for Cat the Cat), peanut butter (for Rocky and Mick) and chocolate spread (for himself).

At the supermarket, SuperBaby's mother brought a

special little seat from the car, which she put on the shopping trolley and strapped SuperBaby into it. She didn't notice that he had a small lump poking out the side of his baby suit (that was Mick), or that the bags she clipped onto the shopping trolley were heavier than the handbag she'd put inside one of them (that was Rocky).

SuperBaby cried when she fastened the trolley straps around him. *He was a prisoner! He hated that!*

'Shhh!' she said crossly. 'You can't cry in here. This is a posh supermarket. We're not in *ASBO* today, we're in *Snobrose*. You'll have to behave!'

But *she* didn't behave. As usual, she kept abandoning him in random places while she walked away to pick things off the shelves. He hated that as well!

He wanted to take things from the shelf too! He wanted to take *everything* from the shelf, squeeze it, sniff it, lick it, bite it and then drop it on the floor. This was a natural baby desire. But his mother didn't understand that.

He promised himself, *'One day I'll break free and zoom up and down the whole shop and play with everything. And I'll eat all the sweets! And I'll be sick on the floor!'*

'Yeah, me too!' said a voice from a shopping bag.

'*Squeak!*' said another.

SuperBaby complained, 'Mummy's walked away from my trolley again. I'm all alone! And there's Strangers all around!'

'So?' asked Rocky.

SuperBaby whispered, 'I read about Strangers in a Good Parents Book that Grandma left on the table one day. Strangers are *Bad*. They Can't be Trusted!'

'Why not?'

'I don't know. Mummy took the book away before I got to that part. She sometimes hides books from me. I had to hide one from *her* because it was about Difficult Babies and it was worrying her!'

'*Squeak!*'

'Mick says maybe Strangers don't wash properly.'

'*Squeak!*'

'Or they say rude words like –'

'*Squeakkk!*'

'– alright, alright Mick – I wasn't gonna say it.'

SuperBaby said, 'When I grow up, I'll catch all the strangers and put them in prison!'

But just now he was trapped in Baby Prison and the strangers were gliding around him like hungry sharks. One man smiled at him as he passed.

Oh no! The book said to never trust a smiling stranger!

One old lady patted him on the head and said he was cute. *That* meant she wanted to kidnap him and take him home to be *her* baby. And she would force him to do the washing and the ironing! He started to cry. He didn't want to do the ironing…

The smiling man came back. He looked all around and then he slipped his hand into one of the shopping bags clipped onto the trolley and –

He was trying to steal Mummy's handbag!

'What a sweet baby!' said the man, bending over towards the baby to hide what he was doing. Then a puzzled look appeared on his face. He pulled his hand out and looked down at what he was holding.

Two beady black eyes looked back at him, above a toothy, whiskery smile. Then the teeth flashed as they went to work on his fingers.

'Aiiiii! Ouch!!!!'

The man dropped Rocky back into the shopping bag and ran out of the shop, holding one very painful hand in the other.

'See?' whispered SuperBaby to his friends. 'I told you strangers are bad!'

The old lady came back, too. 'What a sweet baby you are!' she said. 'Just like my own little baby, so long ago! I do miss him.'

Oh no! A life of ironing and cleaning shoes was on its way!

'Can I give you a kiss?' she asked. 'I'm sure your

mother wouldn't mind!'

Oh, yuk. He didn't want to be kissed by a stranger! He would probably catch Stranger Disease! And she had a mole above her lip, with hairs on it. The hairs were going to be tickly. And maybe she would sneeze at the last moment and spatter him with slobbery bits! Or she might have false teeth and they would fall out onto his head!

He whispered to his friends, 'Save me!'

She bent to kiss him on the cheek. SuperBaby squeezed his eyes tight, tucked his head as low as possible and tried not to think about the tickly mole and diseases and false teeth and flying snot.

'Ouch!' the lady gasped.

Mick had bravely scrambled out of SuperBaby's baby suit onto SuperBaby's shoulder, and had been kissed instead.

'Squeak!' he said in a pleasantly surprised way.

Rocky laughed quietly. 'Mick says dat was his first kiss!' He climbed out of the bag and held up his lips to be kissed next. 'My turn!' he announced.

The lady gasped and scurried away.

'Woss wrong?' Rocky called after her. 'Aren't I good enough for you? You kissed Mick! He's only a mouse!' He grumbled, 'Some people have no taste.'

Another trolley bumped into SuperBaby's. *A stranger who couldn't drive! He should cry for his mother! He* … He looked at the other trolley and was speechless. He was even cryless.

It looked like the girl he had seen on the beach!

A baby girl was in a trolley seat like his own. She had cute blond curls and a tiny nose that turned up a little at the end. She was wearing tiny red shoes, pink socks and a pink lacy dress with ruffles all over it. She was looking at him as if she couldn't believe her eyes. She extended a slender and elegant arm in his direction and pointed with a cute, tiny finger.

Her mother asked, 'You want that one? Awww… Of course you can have it!' Her mother took a step towards SuperBaby and reached towards him.

Oh no! He was going to be babynapped!

But he didn't mind. He would have a cute girl-friend and new toys and a mother who didn't abandon him in supermarkets! Hooray!

The new mother took hold of his trolley. *Yes!*

She pushed it to one side. *What?*

She took a packet of dried baby food from the shelf next to him and gave it to the tiny girl.

No!

The girl put a corner of the box into her mouth and chewed on it thoughtfully while looking at SuperBaby. She took it out of her mouth and held it towards him.

His little heart skipped a beat. Then he heard his own mother's voice as she returned with an armful of shopping: 'How sweet! She likes you!'

SuperBaby replied excitedly, 'Yes! And I'm going to run away with her and we'll live happily ever after and have lots of nice toys and eat special baby food that costs a million gold coins a box!'

But he was so excited that it came out as totally garbled baby gabble, something like '*Ysm gnna rnway wivver nwelve ippy iffrafter nhv…*'

The other mother said, 'Aww! It's almost like he's trying to say words! How old is he?'

'Seven months.'

'So is Maria.'

SuperBaby's heart skipped another beat. They were the same age! They were *made* for each other!

'Maria can say some words already,' said the other mother proudly. 'The other day she said "cat" plain as plain. Say cat, Maria!'

'*Kkt.*'

The mother smiled victoriously. 'Did you hear that? Isn't she amazing? What about your baby? Does he say any real words? Can he say cat?'

'No,' said his mother, looking sad.

Oh no! His mother mustn't be sad! He had to fix this!

'Caterpillar–cataclysm-cinema-catapult-calculator-calligraphy-catastrophe-constellation,' he gabbled in one breath, so that it sounded like one big word.

Both mothers stared at him, shocked. Little Maria

began to cry. *Ooops…* Maybe one of those was a Rude Word?

'Goo?' he said. 'Kk?'

'Aww! He's trying to say it too!' said the other mother; and Maria was beaming at him again.

There was another bump, and a third trolley rudely pushed in between his and Maria's. A new face looked at him from a trolley seat.

It was a big boy – over a year old - with a round face and a roving eye. The boy looked at Maria and made a kissing sound towards her.

Oh, yuk. So common!

But Maria laughed and held out her little hands towards the new boy.

Oh no! She liked him!

'He's such a big boy!' said Maria's mother approvingly.

SuperBaby frowned but made a mental note:

Big must be *Good.* Then he felt like crying, because he knew he wasn't big!

The big baby's mother was big too, and had a big superior smile on her big superior face as she said in a rather smug and self-important voice, 'Yes, dear little Thug has always been advanced for his age. And he's so handsome and clever!' She looked at SuperBaby and added, "Other little boys look rather ugly and stupid and pathetic next to him.'

'Can he say cat?' asked the first mother.

'Say cat, Thug,' prompted his mother.

'Won't!' the boy sulked.

'Isn't he cute?' his mother gushed. 'He has so much character!'

Little Maria was gazing at the boy. 'Won't!' she whispered in wonder. She clapped her hands.

SuperBaby fumed. He had been loved for less than a minute, and had already been rejected for someone older and bigger and ruder. He would show them! He opened his mouth to say something really clever and important and romantic and –

- And then the rude boy stuck a finger in his nose and flicked a bogey at SuperBaby. It splatted on his face! It almost got him in the mouth! *Oh yuk!*

The little girl laughed again, pointing at SuperBaby's bogey-splattered face.

This was terrible!

SuperBaby cried as he wiped bogey goo from his face. He flicked it away... *Oops.* It sailed over the shelf to his right and came down in the next aisle.

'Ow!' someone shouted.

Ah ha! thought SuperBaby. *He could fight the boy with Super Bogey Flicking!* SuperBaby found one and shot it at the horrible Thug. He missed. It hit some cereal in Thug's shopping trolley and made a hole in the box.

He looked for his mother – but she'd wandered off again, chatting with the other two mothers!

Now the little girl was flirting with the new boy. She giggled and flashed her eyes and showed him her cute socks, and even burped at him!

This was war!

SuperBaby had to do something to show he was as good as his thuggish rival! Not bogey flicking this time. He needed something *better* than that!

'Mick?' he whispered. 'Have you got any mouse

poo you can lend me? Rocky?'

'Not just now.'

'*Squeak.*'

'Oh well. I'll have to find something else.'

But what could he use? Baby dribble? Earwax?

He looked in the trolley. Brussels sprouts? Stinky fishy bits from the cat food pouches? Blueberries? Prawns? Butter? Sprouts? Mayonnaise mustard glue shoe polish fizzy drinks custard gravy eggs caviar giblets squids kidneys mushrooms frozen peas?

SuperBaby whispered to his friends, 'I need something slimy and horrible to throw at him!'

Rocky stuck his head out of the shopping bag. 'Nah. You should do *nice* things to bad people.'

'Why?' asked SuperBaby. 'That seems a very silly thing to do!'

Rocky shrugged his furry rat shoulders. 'I don't know why. But I read it in a good book I found at the dump. Try it!'

Nice things… SuperBaby reached into the trolley and pulled out Mummy's box of special chocolates. He opened the box and flicked one to the other boy. It hit him on the nose and dropped into his lap.

'Waaaa!' The boy cried and pointed at SuperBaby. The boy's mother was walking back and saw him pointing. She asked, 'Did the nasty little baby hurt you? Don't let him get away with that! Teach him not to mess with the Fotherington-Snobbies!'

She pushed the trolleys together and her little bruiser began kicking at SuperBaby, but SuperBaby dodged that. The boy drew back his arm to deliver a punch – but he suddenly noticed the chocolate in his lap and stopped to eat it.

'Choc'let!' he crowed. He grabbed the box from SuperBaby's hand. 'More!'

No! They had his mother's chocolate!

SuperBaby tried to take back the box, but the boy's big mother grabbed it first. 'One is enough!' she said, shoving two chocolates into her big mouth and putting the box in her own handbag and walking away.

Her toddler was very angry now.

'Want choc'let!' he howled. He reached into his trolley and grabbed a grape, which he flung at SuperBaby. 'Gotcha!' he gurgled.

Little Maria laughed and clapped her hands.

Little Thug looked pleased with himself. He put a

grape in his mouth and chewed it. Then he took it out and threw the half-eaten grape at SuperBaby too.

'Gotcha 'gain! Ha ha!'

'Gtcha!' echoed Maria, gazing adoringly at the bigger boy.

SuperBaby looked around. All the grownups were busy looking at shelves and lists. He reached into his trolley and found the squeezy bottle of tomato ketchup. He thought about plugging Thug's big mouth with it.

But he had a better idea… He took off the lid and ripped the paper seal from the top. He screwed the lid on again and checked all around him.

'Do nice things!' warned Rocky.

'Nah! Squeak!' Mick disagreed.

'Ketchup *is* nice!' said SuperBaby. 'Hands up who likes ketchup!'

Thug and Maria both raised their hands.

'See? They asked for it!' He squirted ketchup all over them. 'Gotcha!' he shouted.

'Now we're gonna be in trouble!' groaned Rocky.

'Squeak! Runnnn!' squeaked Mick.

SuperBaby threw the empty ketchup bottle into Thug's trolley and stretched his arms forward, as if he was flying. It worked! His trolley slid past the other two, gently pushing them aside. He made the trolley drift away a few lengths, then let it glide to a stop next to some books.

He was studying a book called *Wicked Tales Four* when his mother returned with a weird vegetable, which she dropped into the trolley. *(Why were there so many odd vegetables in the world?* he wondered)

'Aww – how sweet!' she said to him. 'You're pretending to read! And look – there's a cute baby on the cover who looks just like you!'

'*Google super babby boogle?*' he burbled happily. He turned to watch the other two mothers, who were walking back to their own trolleys.

A ratty voice whispered from the shopping bags: 'Five … four … three … two … one … *go!*'

Suddenly there was a shouting of mothers, crying of ketchup-covered babies and waving of an empty plastic ketchup bottle.

'Oh dear,' said SuperBaby's mother. 'What a mess! I'm so glad you weren't involved in that.'

Supermarket Car Park Adventures

Supermarkets are like forests: all manner of wild creatures lurk in the shadows. On the way in, SuperBaby had waved at two hopeful charity collectors and made *BooGahBah!* noises at a man offering to wash their car. Inside the shop, he had fought off two strangers and Thug the Baby Bully. *Now* he and his mother had to cross the car park again, and it was election time: so there would be politicians waiting for them. He prepared his weapons….

SuperBaby's mother was wheeling the supermarket trolley to the car when someone called to her. SuperBaby saw her look up and shake her head at someone.

'Excuse me! Could I have a word?' the voice said.

SuperBaby's mother put her head down and tried to run for the car, but the trolley had one bad wheel and it preferred to go around in circles.

Someone with a big video camera stepped across in front of the trolley. She swerved to miss him and hit the knee of a big man instead.

'Ow!!' The big man hopped about on one leg.

'I'm terribly sorry,' said SuperBaby's mother. 'I didn't mean to hit you. This trolley is useless. It –'

The big man had a large red face, a red neck and a lot of orange-coloured hair. He held out his hand to SuperBaby's mother. She reluctantly shook it; the cameraman recorded the handshake and a woman with a microphone recorded her saying:

'Pardon me, but do I know you?'

'Grump. *The* Grump. Do you live here?'

'I live in Overton. I really don't know you.'

The big man frowned. He waved his big hands a lot as he insisted, 'Of course you do. *Everyone* knows me and my TV show – and my amazing businesses – and my beautiful children - and you *must* know I'm running for Mayor of this fine city.'

'I do?'

'Of course you do. And I know I can count on your vote, because I'm going to change things, and change is always GOOD. *Vote Grump! Make Overton Great Again!*' He gestured around the car park.

She said, 'But this is Newbury.'

His brow furrowed. 'You said it was Overton. We

have video evidence that you said that, just after you tried to break my knee with your trolley.'

SuperBaby's mother said, 'I was trying to take the trolley to the car but it doesn't steer straight and - '

He interrupted, 'When I'm your mayor, I will tighten the law on trolleys. We'll declare war on bad trolleys and destroy them with targeted drone attacks. And we'll imprison everyone who recklessly drives a bad trolley into someone's knees.'

She said, 'I don't see how that would help.'

The man nodded gravely. 'I know it's complicated for a woman to understand. When you get home, you should ask your husband to explain it to you.'

'What? How can you suggest I need to ask him?!'

He said, 'People are often astonished at my plain speaking. But I tell them: We can all see the things that are wrong in this city but only *I* have a plan to fix them. Take the rat problem, for instance.'

'Rat problem? But we don't have -'

'Stop there!' The man shook his head ponderously and SuperBaby saw his hair wobble about on top of it. '*Everyone* knows there's a rat problem.'

'Well, *I* didn't know –'

'I'm sure your husband knows about it; ask him when you get home. He knows the rats are taking over your peaceful home in beautiful Newbury. *Vote Grump! Make Newbury Great Again!*'

'I live in Overton.'

His brow furrowed. 'You keep changing your story about which town this is. Make your mind up!'

She said patiently, 'I *live* in Overton but I *shop* here in Newbury. And Newbury isn't a city, it's a town.'

'I think you need to ask your husband to explain all that to you! But let's turn to the real issue: How do we deal with the rats and their pesky mice friends? My opponent pretends there's no problem. But *we* know, don't we – you and me and your husband?'

'I don't think –' she began.

'Then you shouldn't interrupt! *I have a plan.* We will *bomb* them. And then we'll build a wall to keep the rats out. A *big* wall. And we'll make the other cities around here *pay* for the wall. And if we find any rodents still hiding in our fair city, we'll send those nasty rats and mice over the wall. We'll use slingshots, catapults, cannons and water slides. Haha!'

'You're – ' SuperBaby's mother spluttered.

'- *Bahboocrazy!*' SuperBaby said, then started to cry because they were planning to hurt his friends.

The man looked down at the trolley. 'A baby!' he chortled. 'I *love* babies! Can I pick him up?'

'Please don't –'

'Thank you.' He snatched SuperBaby from the trolley and bounced him about in his arms. He didn't notice that there were a couple of small furry animals clinging to the baby's legs.

'Picture for the newspapers!' he said to the cameraman. He held SuperBaby close to his own face and pursed his lips as if about to kiss him.

SuperBaby decided it was time for his latest superpower: a double-edged raspberry. You do this at both ends of your body at the same time – a super-burp-fart. *POW!*

'Arggh! Disgusting!' groaned the man. 'I *hate* babies!' He gave SuperBaby his special frown, the one that made other people do whatever he ordered.

This scared SuperBaby so much that the baby wet himself… and quite a lot of the wetness spilled out of the nappy, filling the man's hands.

'Horrible creature! Take him back. Catch!'

He tossed SuperBaby to the mother, who panicked and shrieked. SuperBaby corrected his flight for the poor aim of the man and landed gently in his mother's arms.

Meanwhile, the Mayor-to-be was looking with surprise at the animals climbing up his arms.

'Rats!' he shouted. 'They're everywhere!'

Rocky and Mick scampered onto the man's shoulders and leaped upon his head. They tried to do a little dance up there but his fluffy orange hairpiece wasn't well enough attached to resist the boogying of two excited rodents, so it slipped off his head and rolled about the car park with the animals inside it.

'My hair! Give me back my hair!'

He chased them to and fro, trying to stamp on the ball of hair that skipped and bounced always one step ahead. The cameraman kept filming…

The hairball came to rest under a trolley wheel and he snatched it up, shaking Mick and Rocky onto the tarmac and kicking at them.

Bad mistake. Mick ran up one trouser leg and Rocky squeezed into the other. They climbed quickly, crossed over at the top, then started down again.

Turned around at the bottom, climbed again… and so on. The cameraman kept filming…

Mayor-to-be Grump threw down his hairpiece, swatted at his trousers, then released the buckle, un-zipped them and kicked them off. Fortunately, he was wearing underwear.

Fortunately too, it was patriotic underwear, in the pattern of the UK flag. He pointed at his big rear.

'Look at that!' he shouted. 'Salute the flag! Make our country great again! Vote Grump!'

Unfortunately, the underwear was silky with pink frilly edges and clearly made for ladies. It swished in the sunlight as the great man chased two rodents around the car park in his undies, shouting for them to give back the hairpiece that they were playing tug of war with.

The cameraman kept filming….

The Tale of "Bad the Burglar"

Dear Dairy

Yesterday my parents were talking about something in the newspaper. They said there were robbers in the area who break into houses at night and steal people's special things. They called robbers like that Burglars and said they were bad.

I was sad that the burglars are going to take our special things and I cried. Then I made them give me the newspaper to play with and I read about burglars while I was tearing the pages to shreds and throwing the bits in the air and gurgling happily.

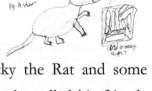

The next morning at nap time, SuperBaby flew to the rubbish dump to collect Rocky the Rat and some cold, greasy chips to eat. Then he called his friends together for a meeting.

'We must protect the house,' SuperBaby said. 'A burglar might come and steal Ben the Box!'

'And our special fries,' said Rocky the Rat, pointing at the big bag of chips they were all eating from, including Connie the Crow.

'My scratching tree,' said Cat the Cat.

'*Squeak!*' said Mick the Mouse.

'What did he say?' asked SuperBaby.

'He says the burglar might steal his tail,' said Rocky the Rat. 'That mouse is crazy.'

'Burglars are Bad,' said SuperBaby. There's no telling what they might steal! But we'll stop him. I read in the newspaper that this burglar comes at night, so we'll keep awake and catch him! Will you help me?'

'*Squeak.*'

Rocky said, 'Mick and I sleep in the day and are awake at night anyway, so we don't mind.'

Cat the Cat shrugged her shoulders. 'I'll do my best,' she yawned. Then she dozed off.

Connie pulled her head out of the bag of chips. 'Can't help

you, kid,' she chirped. 'We crows don't fly about the dark – we'd just bump into things. But I've got a couple of owl friends I could ask. Well, not "friends" exactly, I mean no one's friends with an owl, they're a bit snooty, know what I mean?'

'*Squeak!*' complained an unhappy mouse who was now hiding under a table.

'No owls,' said SuperBaby. 'They make Mick nervous. But we do need some weapons. Rocky - can you find some at that big place we went with Ben the Box? They had lots of scary things there.'

'You mean at the Waste Recycling Centre? Yeah, I'll go ask around tonight…'

Rocky returned at dawn dragging a bag of pineapple fritters, pickled onions, a water pistol and a pellet gun.

'These are great!' said SuperBaby, trying the guns.

'Yes, but we'll have to find something to shoot out of them,' said Cat the Cat.

'Leave it to me!' said the baby.

The next few nights were difficult. SuperBaby tried to act as night watchman but - being a baby - he kept falling asleep. Rocky the Rat and Cat the Cat had to take it in turn to watch, with Mick the Mouse as the runner to take *Squeak!* messages to SuperBaby if a burglar came.

And he did come. He was wearing a woolly hat pulled down to his eyebrows and was carrying a bag to put his loot in. He put a ladder up against the back of the house and climbed quietly to the open window. He put his head inside. There was no sound except the squeaking of a mouse. He smiled to himself.

'Hold it right there!' called a cute baby voice.

The burglar turned on his small flashlight. A baby was standing up in its cot, pointing two guns at him.

'I know who you are!' cried SuperBaby. 'You're Bad the Burglar, come to steal our treasure! Well, you can't have Ben the Box!'

'Or our chips and pickled onions,' said a rat-like voice from a dark corner.

'Or my scratching pole,' something meowed.

'Squeak!'

'He don't want your tail, you daft thing,' said Rocky.

'Squeak! Squeak!'

'Or your whiskers.'

The burglar laughed nastily. 'Heh heh... Those aren't real guns. That one's just a water gun! You can't scare me with *that*.'

'Yeah, but it's full of my wee,' said SuperBaby.

'Oh,' said the burglar, looking nervous.

The baby said, 'I've got a pellet gun too!'

'You have?' asked the burglar, looking even more nervous. 'What's in that?'

'Well, I've got poo from Rocky the Rat and Mick the Mouse, and bits from Cat the Cat as well!'

The burglar said, 'That won't stop me! Heh heh...' Still laughing quietly to himself, he started to climb over the window sill.

The baby fired both guns.

'Yukkkkk!' cried the burglar, who really shouldn't have been laughing nastily with his mouth open. He fell off the ladder and ran away.

But the next night he was back.

SuperBaby and his friends were waiting. The baby pointed his guns again and warned him to leave. 'It's serious this time, Bad the Burglar!' he shouted.

The burglar laughed nastily again. He turned his

small flashlight onto his own face. 'Look!' he said. 'I'm wearing a face mask and goggles. Why should I be scared of you? Heh heh heh....'

'I'll bite holes in your car tyres,' said a rat voice from behind the curtains.

'I'll dig up the flowers in your garden,' said a cat voice from the bin beneath the window.

'*Squeakity squeak!*'

SuperBaby said, 'And Mick the Mouse says he'll come round to your house and squeak at you in

the middle of the night and wake you up. *Every single night.* It'll drive you nuts!'

The burglar said, 'I'm still not scared.'

SuperBaby fired his guns.

'Oh, yuk!' said the burglar. 'What's in those?'

'Baby sick!' laughed SuperBaby. 'And there's plenty more where that came from!'

The burglar wiped his face mask and took out a gun of his own. A real gun.

'Back off, Baby!' he ordered.

'I've got lots of other friends to scare you with!' said SuperBaby, grabbing things to throw at the burglar. 'Here's Pam the ping pong ball... (*bip!*), Ted the toy tractor (*bink!*), Ollie the octopus (*bop!*).

The burglar laughed again - cruelly this time, as well as nastily. 'Heh heh! You'll have to do better than that, Baby! I'm coming in!' He began to climb through the window.

'Here's another friend,' said SuperBaby. 'Meet Rick the Brick! Get his toes, Rick!'

Whack!

The brick hit the burglar on his head, knocking him out the window and all the way to the ground. Bad the Burglar was so upset that he gave up being a burglar and became an investment banker instead.

Christmas One: Santa's Grotto

Your first Christmas is special. So much happens that you've never come across before:

✳ There are pretty lights and packages and Christmas carols.

✳ A tree appears inside the house.

✳ There's far too much food to eat.

✳ Your relatives visit a lot, laugh a lot and sometimes argue a lot.

✳ A fat, white-bearded man dressed in red turns up and says *Ho Ho Ho* all the time.

SuperBaby was taken to see the big man, whose name was Santa and also Father Christmas.

His mother said as they were driving into town, 'Santa takes presents to all the good children. He puts the presents in a big sleigh and flies around the world delivering them at Christmas.'

His father said, 'And you've been a good boy, so *you'll* get lots of presents.'

SuperBaby began to cry. He was sad for the children who hadn't been good enough and wouldn't be getting any presents. Also, he was worried that there wouldn't be room on the sleigh for the thousand presents he must have earned by now.

His mother said, 'Stop crying! Babies who cry all the time don't get *any* presents.'

SuperBaby cried harder. It always upset him when his parents talked about bad things happening, especially if those bad things depended on him not doing something that babies can hardly control.

His father tried a different approach: 'If you stop crying, Santa will give you a sweetie!'

SuperBaby stopped crying and thought about this. He liked the idea of sweets. But maybe his parents shouldn't be encouraging him to take sweets from strangers!

Someone had screened off part of the shopping mall with white curtains and carpets, making it look like a big snowy mountain with a doorway opening into it. There was a big sign over the doorway:

SANTA'S GROTTO

To one side of the doorway, there was a big wood-

CHRISTMAS ONE: SANTA'S GROTTO

en sleigh loaded with bright packages in mysterious shapes. A sign on the sleigh announced:

YOUR CHILD COULD WIN A PRESENT!

There was a special train that took you inside the grotto. The train was shaped like a sleigh too, and had an engine that looked like a fat, square reindeer.

SuperBaby's father bought one Santa's Grotto train ticket from a smiling Elf lady. SuperBaby had been told about Elves: they helped Santa. This one was helping him by taking a lot of money from people and putting it into a big leather bag.

The Elf lady had pointy ears that looked plastic. They had slipped down her head and were pointing sideways, as if she was a lop-eared rabbit. She said to his parents:

'Congratulations! Your name will be entered in Santa's Sweepstake and your child can win one of the wonderful presents in the sleigh. Also, Santa will send your little boy a special Santa's Christmas Card. Please write your name and address in Santa's Big Book of Good Boys and Girls.'

She paused and asked dramatically, '*Has* he been a good boy this year?'

SuperBaby saw his father and mother exchange glances. He had a moment of panic. *Did they suspect he was borrowing the jar of chocolate spread from time to time?*

'Of course he's a good boy!' his parents chorused. 'He's the best boy in the world!'

SuperBaby's little heart thumped with joy!

SuperBaby's father wrote his address in the book while SuperBaby stared at the wonderful sleigh. Maybe he would win ALL the presents!

The Elf pointed at the book again and whispered, 'If you're going away for Christmas, please write down the days you'll be away, so we can deliver the card and present when you're still at home.'

SuperBaby's father did this too.

They boarded the magical train and glided slowly – *too slowly!* – across to the magical mountain and through the dark doorway. The train wound in and out of dark twisty passages before emerging into a lighted cavern.

A second elf was waiting at the end of the train line. This one was short and plump, and his big elf ears were pointing the right way. He opened the doors of the train and led them to what looked like a small cave.

SuperBaby had to wait in line with three other children. They were being rather noisy and he decided they wouldn't be getting any presents from Santa. Especially the one who kept picking his nose and eating the bogeys!

Finally SuperBaby was led inside the cave and he saw Santa up close for the first time, seated on a magnificent padded chair. He wasn't as big as the pictures SuperBaby had seen, but he *did* have a white Santa beard, little glasses, a big tummy and a suit of red and white fur. He was looking at a piece of paper in his hand.

Ho Ho Ho!' he called. 'Come sit on my knee, little – um – (*he looked at the paper again*) boy!'

SuperBaby was lifted by his mother onto Santa's knee. It was a very bony knee.

Santa's tummy was the right size, but a funny shape: it was the sort of tummy you would get if you stuffed a pillow under a big furry jacket. His face was a bit red, as if the jacket was too warm. His white beard was big and lovely but –

Poor Santa! He had a beard disease! It was peeling off his face on one side! SuperBaby began to cry.

'Ho Ho Ho! What do you want for Christmas?'

SuperBaby stopped crying. This was the most important question he had ever been asked. He thought hard. He didn't want to use his first official word yet,

✕ CHRISTMAS ONE: SANTA'S GROTTO ✕

but he didn't want to miss out on the best Christmas presents of all time either. Maybe he would get a hundred of them. *Maybe a million!*

'Sweets?' asked Santa. 'Toys? Maybe a big car like your daddy's? A little book? A game to play? Whisper in Santa's ear, my child!'

There was something familiar about Santa's voice. And Santa's face reminded SuperBaby of a face he'd seen before, but he couldn't remember where.

Santa pointed at the paper he was holding. 'I have a list of Good Children written here! Ho ho ho! Are you on it? Let me see…. Hmmm… I know all the good children in this town… Are you little Sylvester? And do you live at 13 Dellands?'

SuperBaby nodded. This was wonderful! Santa knew his name and his house!

'13 Dellands…' repeated Santa softly. He looked closely at SuperBaby. The hand that held the list began to shake. The friendly Santa eyes turned as hard and cold as the fake icicles hanging in his grotto.

He said briskly, 'Make your mind up! Toys, chocolates, sweets, teddies, dollies, bricks – I mean, *books*. What do you want, boy?'

✕ 183 ✕

SuperBaby stretched up and whispered into Santa's ear, making his voice small so that his parents wouldn't hear and be upset that the first word they heard from him wasn't something cute like "Mama".

'Everything!' he whispered. 'I want *everything* on the sleigh!'

'Excellent,' said Santa through clenched teeth, in a voice no longer full of Ho Ho Ho. 'You can have *everything*. I'll bring it to you the night before Christmas. Off you go now!'

Then he put his mouth very close to SuperBaby's ear and whispered back, 'You're a very bad boy and you'll get nothing. *Nothing!*'

SuperBaby knew that voice. It was the voice of Bad the Burglar.

This was dreadful. Bad the Burglar was pretending to be Santa! But why? As the magical train took them out of Santa's kingdom, SuperBaby's detective brain began to work it out....

Maybe the burglar had crept into the Grotto early that morning and tried to steal the sleigh with all the toys on it. Maybe he had stolen Santa himself, and was going to hold him for ransom! But maybe it had taken longer that the burglar expected - and then the children started turning up, so Bad the Burglar had to pretend to be Santa for a day.

Tonight he would get away, and no one would ever see Santa again. There would be no more Christmas presents, ever. *Oh no!*

'I must stop Bad the Burglar!' SuperBaby said to himself.

'What?' asked his mother.

'Boppy baddy burger bar,' SuperBaby said hastily.

As they were getting off the train, he looked back at Santa's Grotto, with its lovely welcoming sign.

People needed to be warned!

He peered at the sign again. It was made out of individual letters hung on nails. And if he got up there and changed the letters around... *yes!*

But everyone would see him. He needed a diversion. He needed everyone to be looking in the other direction. But how?

Some super powers appear to be rather useless, even if they're fun. SuperBaby could flick a bogey at high speed. He could spit from his window all the way across the road (he knew that because he had tried it last week and accidentally hit the postman). And he could blow out candles on the other side of a room. What if –

The Elf Lady was talking to a new group of families. Her pointy ears were flopping all over the place. One SuperBlow, and the ears went flying across the room. Another puff, and her dress flapped up and wrapped about her head, showing her pink and green stripy tights.

She screamed. Everyone turned to look.

SuperBaby slipped his hand from his mother's and flew up to the sign. His little hands moved in a blur. Two seconds later he was back with his mother.

He looked back as they walked out of the Mall. Yes, he had done it right. The sign now read:

SANTA'S GOT ROT.

When he got home, SuperBaby called a meeting of all his friends. Connie the Crow perched on the window ledge, Cat the Cat purred at his feet in the cot, and Mick and Rocky were spinning around on the wire mobile of the planets above his bed (Mick was clinging nervously to the Earth and Rocky was chuckling from Jupiter).

SuperBaby announced, 'Santa has been kidnapped and Bad the Burglar has taken his place!' He told them about his meeting at Santa's Grotto.

The animals listened quietly, then exchanged glances. Finally, Cat the Cat spoke:

'Santa isn't real.'

'Or Father Christmas,' said Connie the Crow.

'Or the Elves,' said Rocky.

'Squeak?' asked Mick.

'Nah, Mick, the Mouse Fairy isn't real either.'

'Squeak....'

'Aw, don't cry, Mick.'

SuperBaby started crying too.

SIENNA

'What's wrong, kiddie?' asked Connie the Crow.

SuperBaby sobbed, 'I won't get any presents! *Nobody* will get any presents!'

'Don't be daft,' said the Cat. 'You'll get presents from your mum and dad and friends and family. They just pretend the presents come from Santa.'

SuperBaby asked, 'There's really no Santa?'

'Nah.'

'What about the Easter Bunny?'

'Nah.'

'*Squeak!*'

'Mick says he's heard about a gang of seven Easter Bunnies that go around shooting Easter Eggs at people,' Rocky said. 'That might be true.'

SuperBaby asked, 'What about the baby Jesus?'

'He's real.'

'Yeah.'

'Of course.'

'*Squeak!*'

Rocky said, 'My great-great-great a thousand times grandma got her tail stepped on by a wise man that came to see the baby Jesus.'

SuperBaby thought about this for a while. 'But why is Bad the Burglar pretending to be Santa?'

'Because humans are crazy!' the others chorused.

SuperBaby shook his head. 'Maybe he has a bad plan. But I don't see what it can be…'

'Use your detective brain,' suggested the crow. 'You said your dad told the Elves where you live.'

'Oh no!' exclaimed SuperBaby. 'He also told them what days we'll be away from the house. That's not a good thing to tell a burglar!'

'*Ooooopsqueak!*' said Mick.

Christmas Two: Babynapped

SuperBaby was just a baby, so he didn't know that people can be really, really bad. He wouldn't have guessed that as soon as Bad the Burglar had taken off his Santa suit, he held a meeting in his office with two people who had recently been dressed as Elves.

'As you know,' began Bad the Burglar, 'I gave up

being a Burglar and became an Investment Banker instead. Being a Banker pays the bills, but it isn't as fun as being a Burglar.'

He sighed. 'That's why I planned our little Santa Scam. I thought it would be enough to keep me happy. But something happened today: something *terrible!* So I have a *new* plan. A plan for *Revenge...*'

'What's in it for us?' asked Lady Beatrice, who was posh and tall and very thin, and had been the first Elf that SuperBaby saw.

'Yeah. Wotsinnit fer us?' asked her husband Sir Bertie, who wasn't posh, wasn't tall and was shaped rather like a beach ball. He was the second Elf.

'A lot of money,' said Bad the ex-Burglar Banker.

'We *do* need money,' sniffed Lady B. 'Things have been rather tight since Daddy got sent to prison.'

Sir B rubbed his hands together. 'Lotsa money? Dat's good. How much?'

'I can offer you a hundred thousand.'

Sir B started counting on his fingers, but gave up. He said, 'Wow.... And waddawe gotta do?'

'Just kidnap a baby.'

Lady B frowned. 'So *we* get a hundred grand... but

what do *you* get out of it?'

'Revenge!' shouted Bad the Banker. 'That little beast has ruined my vertical life!'

'Yer wot?'

Bad the Banker rose from his enormous, expensive desk and paced up and down his enormous, expensive Investment Banker's office. 'I used to like heights. I climbed trees, flew planes, skied down snowy slopes, strolled up grassy hills. Now I can't climb a ladder or even stand on a chair. If I do, I imagine… *toys.*'

'Toys?' asked the posh voice.

'Olly the Octopus, Pam the Ping Pong Ball, Ted the Toy Tractor. I dream of them at night and imagine them all day. I see them flying through the air at my face. And then, as I dodge their hideous flying shapes, I see something behind them, moving fast, homing in on me like a missile: my nemesis.'

'Nems… missus?' asked the other voice. 'Wozzat?'

'My *doom:* Rick the Brick. With his green curly hair and scary crayon smile. He whacks me right on the forehead. And I'm falling, falling, falling….'

Bad the Banker hurried back to his seat and sat

down, gripping the edge of his desk as if he was afraid of falling through the floor into a deep pit. His voice shook.

'I want you to kidnap that baby. I want you to steal all his toys and put them in a big hole and cover them with a million tons of gravel. I want you to make him cry. Don't read him any bedtime stories or play games with him. Tell him he's a Bad Baby. Tell him he's ugly and his baby clothes are out of fashion. Tell him he's no good at goo-gooing. Tell him everyone hates him and the girl babies won't ever kiss him. Tell him he smells like a pig. And then...'

'Then?' asked Sir and Lady B together.

'When the baby has cried for several days and says he's sorry, we'll get his parents to pay us a ransom. And then we'll leave the baby somewhere really scary, like maybe on top of a big roller coaster. That'll serve him right!'

'Yea, dat'll do it.'

'Indubitably.'

Early one morning soon after this, SuperBaby's mother went to the baby's cot and found... nothing.

No baby, no toys, not even Ben the Box. Stuck to the cot with a piece of duct tape was a note written on a piece of paper torn out of a colouring book. It was written by two different hands:

~~We got yer baby~~

We have your baby. We will contact you later for a ransom.

~~Yeah an you betta pay up qwick or else~~

You will receive full instructions later. Until then –

Keep yer moufs shut!

Exactly so. Do not communicate with the police.

~~Or talk to dem.~~

That's the same thing, you nitwit.

Who are you callin a nitwit?

SuperBaby's mother screamed, and the father came running.

'I didn't do it!' he said as he reached the doorway. 'It wasn't my fault… whatever it was!'

And for the first time ever, she agreed with him.

The first stage of babynapping had gone smoothly.

When Bad the Burglar's helpers sneaked in through the window in the middle of the night, they found SuperBaby sound asleep, dreaming of an enormous sleigh full of the best presents in the world.

His friends were asleep, too. SuperBaby had spent the evening making a big mountain of cuddly toys in the middle of the room and they'd all had a great game of burrowing into the mountain, leaping onto it from the top of the wardrobe, rolling down it, and throwing one another onto it.

Mick, Rocky and Cat the Cat were snoozing in amongst the toys when the short, round burglar shoved everything into a couple of large black sacks and carried them away.

The tall, thin lady burglar wrapped SuperBaby in a blanket and stepped quietly down the ladder holding the baby.

The second stage was a bit noisier. SuperBaby had woken in a strange car. He was wrapped in a strange blanket and was looking up through the darkness at a face that reminded him of a tall lady Elf he had seen in Santa's grotto. He was so scared that he was sick on the lady's lap.

'Horrid child!' the lady shouted. She wiped herself off with the blanket and put SuperBaby on the floor, where he began to howl.

'Serves you right!' she said, throwing the smelly blanket over him and putting her feet on him to hold him down.

He continued to cry. The car stopped at a traffic light. *Hooray! Someone would hear him!*

He cried louder. *Yes! Any moment now someone would knock on the car window and ask the Elf lady why she was squashing a baby with her hard shoes!*

No. The lady turned on the radio and whizzed up the volume, so that some woman's loud singing drowned his baby cries. (This must be what his parents called Opera. It was full of people making funny noises in a different language).

The lights changed and they drove on. SuperBaby stopped crying. He said to himself:

'Maybe this is a dream and I'll wake up in my cot. Or maybe these are Bad People who turn babies into sausages. Or this is Baby's Got Factor X Talent and they want to take me to Hollywood and make me a superstar. Whatever it is, I

won't *let them win!'*

He stuck his head out of the blanket and was sick on the lady's shoes.

'Gotcha!' he gurgled.

A little later, the car turned into a long, curving drive and parked in front of a big house. The car door next to SuperBaby opened and a Lady Elf voice said sharply as the lady stepped out:

'Bertie, you can bring the baby in. I'm going to change my clothes and wash myself!'

The man in the driving seat said, 'But what about the bags, Beatrice?' His voice was rather like the voice of the chubby Man Elf in Santa's grotto.

The lady shouted back over her shoulder as she stamped away, 'Throw them into the pit after you've dealt with the baby!'

Hard, rough hands wrapped the blanket tightly around SuperBaby and lifted him from the car. He felt himself being carried somewhere. For a moment he thought about flying away. But then he thought, *'No! I need to find out what's going on!'*

The man walked into the big house.... up several flights of stairs... opened a door... flicked a light switch on… then shook SuperBaby out of the blanket into a baby cot with high sides.

'You stay there, sunshine!' he commanded. 'I'll be back once I've dealt with your toys! And you'd better behave. You don't mess with Sir B and Lady B!'

The light was switched off and the door was slammed shut. Heavy footsteps plodded away down the stairs again.

SuperBaby laughed. He flew to the window, opened it, and flew out.

Sir B got to the bottom of the stairs and wiped his hot, sweaty face. 'Them stairs is too many for me!' he exclaimed as he opened the fridge door and found something cool to drink.

Several minutes later he was singing to himself as he walked out to the car. 'And down will come baby, cradle and all!' he crooned. 'Ha ha! And a hundred grand! Loadsa money!'

He opened the rear of the car and pulled out two big black bags. If he'd been looking carefully through the half-darkness, he would have noticed that one bag was wriggling somewhat…

He carried the bags away, whistling. He didn't see a baby shape flying behind him. He was still whistling as he threw the bags into a big hole in the back yard. He didn't hear the annoyed squeaking and meowing from one sack. He also didn't see a baby shape fly down into the hole and start untying the sacks.

He went back to the house and found another cold drink from the fridge. He sat at the table drinking it and trying out new verses for his song.

'*And down will fall baby, toys and all!* No, that doesn't include the money. Uh…. *Rock a bye baby, up in the cot. When the Burglar pays, the toys will… uh… bot… grot… rot? When the parents pay, the cradle shall fall… ummm…*'

Lady B came into the kitchen and shouted at him, 'Bertie! Take that baby upstairs!'

'I did that already, my love,' he said.

'No you didn't! I can see him still in the car!'

She dragged her husband by the ear to the window and pointed outside. SuperBaby was bouncing up and down on the driver's seat of the car, pretending to drive it. He was turning the wheel from side to side and making loud car noises.

'See?' she asked. 'You're so useless, Bertie!'

He grumbled, 'But I *did* bring him in. I put him in the cot upstairs.'

'Nonsense! You always do this to me. You promise to do things but never get round to them.'

He looked at her suspiciously. He said, 'You brought him down again, didn't you? You're messin' wiv my head, right?'

She glared at him. 'Go get the baby, Bertie!' she commanded, pointing out the window.

Catching the baby wasn't as easy to do this time. SuperBaby scooted in and out of the car seats and wriggled loose every time Sir B tried to snatch him. The man was especially puzzled that the baby had some toys now, which he threw very accurately. He even hit Sir B on the nose with Tina the Truck.

Sir B carried SuperBaby inside again, and Lady B came upstairs with him to make sure he did everything right. 'Where did you put the cot for the baby?' she asked as they walked up the stairs.

'In the office on the top floor,' said her husband.

'You silly man!' she fussed. 'All our important papers are in there! And the computer!'

'You're the silly one, not me. Woss he gonna do? Eat the papers? Log onto the computer?'

SuperBaby heard this and giggled. He liked playing on computers!

Lady B shuddered. 'I don't like it when he laughs. It's as if he knows something we don't.'

The cot not only had high sides; it also had a mesh top that Sir B now fastened down with snaps so that the baby couldn't climb out. SuperBaby cried when they put him in it, and Lady B hurried away with her fingers in her ears.

SuperBaby continued to cry while Sir B sat at the computer and typed something very slowly, using one finger. He cried louder and louder, until…

'That's enough, Bad Baby!' the man shouted. He rose from the desk and left the room, slamming the door behind time.

SuperBaby giggled to himself. *This was such fun!*

A crow landed on the window ledge and cawed at him. SuperBaby popped open the top of the cot and wriggled out. He flew to the window and sat on the ledge next to the bird.

'I like this game!' he exclaimed.

'It's more fun than sitting on eggs,' Connie the Crow agreed. 'You can get really bored doing that. And once them eggs hatch, you spend all day stuffin' food into the babies' beaks. That can get on your nerves, too. No time to go the cinema.'

'Crows don't go to the cinema!' SuperBaby said.

'Yeah, but that's only 'cause we don't have time. I can't get babysitters. Except for the cuckoos, they're always offering to help out. But they keep leavin' their own eggs in the nest, and when those hatch, their babies push your own kids out.'

'I'll babysit for you!' SuperBaby promised. 'Let's do a swap – if you'll be my lookout today, I'll look after your babies one evening next week.'

'Awww, that'd be great!' the crow cawed. 'I'll teach you how to feed 'em. You gotta hold the worm in your mouth the right way. It ain't as easy as it looks.'

'I'll do lots of practising,' SuperBaby promised.

SuperBaby opened the office door so that Connie the Crow could fly out and began her Lookout duties. She perched on the stair rail and peered downstairs with her little head held to one side.

SuperBaby hurried to the computer and poked at the keyboard. He read the email that Sir B had been writing. Then he clapped his baby hands with joy.

"Dear Mummy

I hope you'll be proud of your boy Bertie: We've got a baby now! Heh heh, not the way most people get 'em: we had to nick the little monster outta his cot.

If all goes well, we'll get a hundred thousand smackaroos from Bad the Investment Banker wot used to be a Burglar.

He's a cute baby but he almost broke my nose with a toy truck. And he was sick all over Lady B's dress. So we ain't sorry we've gotta hand him back after we get the ransom.

What with the baby and the sleigh full of presents we're gonna sell in London and the houses on Santa's list we're gonna visit when the families are out (wink, wink!), I think it's gonna be a Merry Christmas. We might even be able to get Aunty Mabel outta prison.

Heh heh heh.

More later. The baby's crying and it's doing my head in."

Connie the Crow fluttered back into the room and perched on the desk. She reported, 'The man's asleep on the couch in the front room and the lady's watching TV,' she said. 'What're you doing?'

SuperBaby pointed at the computer screen. 'Those are called *words*,' he explained. 'It's like talking but with scribbles instead.'

'Yeah? And?'

'The words say he's kidnapped me. And he's going to take all the presents on Santa's sleigh and sell them. *And* he's going to burgle lots of houses.'

Connie put her head near the screen and listened. 'It ain't sayin' a thing to me,' she said. 'Just hums a bit.'

SuperBaby explained, 'The words only say things inside your head. You have to look at them and learn what they're saying first. And then you can send your own words to other people.'

'Like, who?'

'Everybody! We can use something called Fakebook. Mummy uses it a lot. You use Fakebook to *pretend* things. You put nice pictures of yourself and your family on it and tell everyone how wonderful you are. You even pretend to have friends on it. And *they* pretend to be *your* friends. It's a lot of fun!'

SuperBaby poked at the keyboard. 'This is how I've seen Mummy do it. You *Share* things. Like this letter. There! I've shared it with everybody. And I can even send it to Mummy's Fakebook. I just type in *Mummy*… oops, that doesn't work. Maybe I can use her other names. I can't remember them all but I'll put in the name that comes on letters the postman brings. Look: there's her picture! Done it.'

'Nice picture of you there,' said Connie, looking at the screen.

'I've got more of me! Mummy made up a Fakebook account just for me. My name is S-Baby and my password is Mummy. See? She writes things that aren't true like "I'm having a lovely time in the park!" and "I love eating my sprouts!".'

Connie shook her head. 'Bad mama,' she said.

SuperBaby started typing on his Fakebook page.

I have been kidnapped by two Elves called Sir Bee and Lady Bee. Please can my mummy and daddy rescue me? Or if they are too busy as usual then another mummy and daddy will do. If I get a new mummy can I have one who doesn't abandon me in the middle of shops while she talks to other mummies? PS I didn't have good time in the park. I had a horrid time because I stepped in some dog poop. And I do NOT like sprouts and never have!'

Just then they heard footsteps coming up the stairs. SuperBaby turned off the computer and flew back into his cot.

The door opened. A face peeked in. SuperBaby threw a ball he'd found in his cot. It bounced off Sir B's nose.

'Ouch!' shouted Sir B. 'You're a very bad baby!' He crossed to the cot and fastened the top again. Then he went downstairs to find another nice drink.

Half an hour later he entered one of their many living rooms in a better mood, but found his wife in a worse one.

'You're so useless!' she shouted at him. 'You can't even put a baby to bed properly!'

Sir B said, 'He *is* in bed! The little beast hit me wiv a ball but I showed him who's boss! He'd pushed the lid off his cot, but I fastened it again.'

'Nitwit! He's right there!' She pointed.

SuperBaby was sitting by the television, posting

bits of baby biscuit into the slot of the DVD player. As Sir B crossed the floor to grab him, SuperBaby picked up a toy metal bus and waved it.

'Goo!' he shouted cheerfully.

Sir B stopped dead and put one hand over his sore nose. He turned to his wife. 'Perhaps *you* oughta put him to bed dis time. A woman's touch, right?'

'I hate babies.'

'You're just bovvered cos he was sick on you.'

Lady B glared at the baby. 'He did it on purpose!'

'Goo!' said SuperBaby, waving the bus again before trying to stuff it inside the music centre.

Lady and Sir B jumped on him together and took the toy away. SuperBaby cried.

'Excellent!' said Lady B. 'Tears and howls! Hold him up while I video it on my phone for Bad the B.'

She pulled a diamond-studded phone from a diamond-studded handbag and recorded the crying.

'Now for a close up… hold him tight… that's it – Euuuugh! He's vomited all over my phone! And my hands! It's dripping down my sleeves!'

'Gotcha three times!' gurgled SuperBaby.

'Did he just say – ?'

'Gobba bee bimes!' SuperBaby corrected himself.

'You'd better go clean that off,' said Sir B.

Lady B went to wash while Sir B kept hold of the baby. He shut all the living room doors, checked the windows and then put SuperBaby on the carpet.

He wagged a finger at the baby. 'Don't you try any tricks with me! If you do, I'll – Come back here!'

SuperBaby had scooted behind one of the sofas and started pulling all the plugs from the electrical sockets. Sir B couldn't reach him from the side of the sofa, so he climbed onto it and leaned over the back to grab the baby and…

… When Lady B returned, Sir B was trapped under the sofa that had somehow fallen on top of him. SuperBaby had taken the flowers out of a vase and was pouring water onto Sir B's head, which was sticking out of one end of the upturned sofa. All the electrical wires had been tied in a big knot, and half the books had come off the bookshelves.

'Bad Baby!' she screamed.

'Gooble wingbing popplepoo!' the baby gurgled.

Lady B carried SuperBaby upstairs, holding him at arm's length so he couldn't be sick on her again. She put him into his cot, threw a blanket over him, fastened the mesh top and stormed out, slamming the door behind her.

She stood outside the door a moment, then knelt and peered through the keyhole. The baby seemed to be asleep. She tiptoed downstairs....

Christmas Three: Playing Games

One very good Christmas tradition is to play some games. SuperBaby loved games…

He flew out the window and glided into a big oak tree outside, seating himself on a branch next to Cat the Cat.

'This is fun!' he said.

'Not for me,' said Cat the Cat. 'They put me in a big bag with your toys. Then they threw the bag into their car. Then they dragged the bag into the back garden and threw it in a big, muddy hole, and *then* threw a second bag on top of it. I was in that bag for a long time until you untied it.'

'I'm sorry,' said SuperBaby. 'Big hug!' He gave the cat a hug, and they both fell out of the tree.

Fortunately they landed on the bags of toys. Unfortunately, some of the toys were hard and pointy.

Fortunately, there were some soft things like Green Teddy mixed in with them.

Unfortunately, there were also some soft things like Rocky and Mick still dozing inside.

'*Squeak!*'

'Owwww!'

'Sorry. Big hug?'

'Nah.'

'*Squeak please!*'

Rocky and Mick crawled out of the bag and sat in SuperBaby's lap while Cat the Cat prowled about.

'We've gotta get home,' said Rocky.

'Not yet!' said SuperBaby. 'It's fun here!'

'Your mother will worry about you,' said the cat.

SuperBaby shook his head. 'No she won't. She loses me at the supermarket a lot. She'll just wonder where she's left me this time.'

Rocky said, 'Maybe your dad will worry.'

'No. He'll be watching television. He never worries

about anything except when there's lots of men kicking a ball on the television. He gets really upset then. Maybe he doesn't want the ball to get hurt.'

'*Squeak!*'

Rocky said, 'Mick says humans are crazy. Except maybe you.'

'We need an escape plan,' said Cat the Cat.

'We need to save the toys first!' said SuperBaby.

'Yeah. Fly that bag somewhere safe.'

SuperBaby pouted. 'But that's not fun enough.'

'*Squeak!*'

'Mick says he's got a good idea…'

Later that morning, Sir and Lady B crossed the lawn wearing rubber boots and carrying gardening tools. They looked down into the big hole.

'Wots all dis?'

Sir B had dragged two big black sacks full of toys to the hole; now only one sack was there, and it was empty… except for…. They opened it carefully.

Lady B said sharply, 'There's just the green teddy inside. What did you do with the other toys?'

'Me, love? I ain't done nuffink. *You* musta done it.'

'I don't find your little pranks funny, Bertie. I never have. They are *always* stupid and childish – just like you. Go get the toys and put them back in the hole.'

'Yeah, yeah: you fink you're so clever. Well, I'm not bitin', Beatrice. You're rubbish at playin' tricks, I can always see through you. You can't even tell jokes properly. So I *know* you've done this. You probably got the gardener to sneak in and nick the toys.'

'No, Bertie. It won't do you any good pretending. Stop this silly game at once!'

'Wot game? I – *Wotzat?*'

He pointed into the branches above them. All the toys were there, huddled into nooks and forked branches, peering worriedly through the leaves.

'Very funny, Bertie - I *don't* think!' Lady B threw down her spade and strode back to the house, her head held high and proud.

Sir B grumbled as he watched her go. 'Play tricks on me, will you? Well, *two* can play that game....'

He went inside and spent a long time collecting all her shoes and carrying them upstairs into the bathtub on the third floor. They half-filled the tub. Then he turned on the bath tap and watched as the shoes began to float. He laughed to see them spinning about in the current.

When he came downstairs again, whistling happily to himself, Lady B was stirring something in a big saucepan on the stove.

'What's for lunch?' asked her husband, patting his large stomach. 'We having shoes? – I mean soup?'

'Leftover vegetable soup.'

'I don't like vegetable shoop... I mean soup.'

'Too bad! Soup for you and me. Bread and water for the horrid baby. Go change his nappy, then bring him down for his lunch.'

'He might hit me on the nose again. And it's your turn to change –'

'Would you like *me* to hit you on the nose instead?' Lady B picked up the ladle she'd been stirring the soup with. She shook it at Sir B, splattering him with soup. He hurried away.

A few moments later he called downstairs, 'The baby's gone!'

She ran upstairs with the ladle still in her hand, dripping soup on every step.

'The window's open!' she shouted, pointing. 'You

left the window open!'

'It wasn't me.'

She shook the ladle at him. 'Stop playing tricks!'

He wiped soup from his face. 'You're the only one playing tricks.'

'No, it's you!'

'Nah, it's you!'

'Or … or someone's babynapped him.'

He shook his big head. 'Don't be silly, girl. Nobody babynaps a baby that's been napped already.'

There was a loud cry from the other side of the house. It sounded like a baby outside. The kidnappers ran from the room and crossed to the big window on the landing where they found…

… toys pressed up against the glass, peering in.

'They're alive! The toys are alive!'

Sir and Lady B ran downstairs, she screaming and he trying to scream, but too plump and out of breath for the scream to come out. They ran into the kitchen. The pot was boiling over on the stove. Its lid was sticking up, as if something didn't quite fit inside it.

Lady B crossed slowly to the stove, her hair on end, her eyes wide in horror. With a trembling hand, she poked the pot lid with the ladle until the lid tumbled off onto the floor.

There was more than vegetable soup in the pot now. What was poking out was not a vegetable. It had fur and a head. Through the steam they could see its staring, lifeless eyes. Green eyes.

'It's the green teddy!'

Lady B turned off the stove and they hurried outside in their slippers to search for the baby. If they had looked up rather than down, they might have noticed a flying baby following above them.

'Baby! Come here, baby!'

'Come 'ere, you little beast!'

They poked their heads into bushes and looked under the cars parked on the drive.

'What about the garage?'

They opened the doors of the garage. Inside it was the sleigh that SuperBaby had first seen outside Santa's grotto. It was still loaded with presents.

'No baby here!' called Sir B, peering under the sleigh while Lady B checked behind it.

Sir B chuckled as he shut the garage door. 'Poor little kiddies. No presents for *them!* But plenty of money for us!'

His wife said, 'Let's go back to the house. The baby must be inside somewhere. He can hardly toddle about, after all. It's not as if he could fly!'

There was a giggle from somewhere overhead.

They went in through the kitchen door. Lady B stopped and pointed at the stove.

'Where's the teddy gone?'

The pot lid was lying on the floor and the pot was empty, except for soup.

'I don't know anything about that, dear,' her husband answered.

They walked into the hallway.

Lady B stopped again and pointed upwards.

'Why is water dripping from upstairs?'

'Oops. I... ah... I don't know anything about that *either*, dear.'

Lady B's phone rang. 'It's Bad the B,' she said. 'I expect it's about the ransom.'

She listened for a few seconds, then turned to her husband and asked:

'Why did you post all our plans on Fakebook?'

'I... ah... don't know anything about that either.'

And then they heard a sound that isn't the best for a kidnapper to hear: a police siren.

They ran outside, where a crowd of toys were lined up outside the kitchen door, watching them.

They screamed and ran for the car. They pulled at the door handles, then ran inside for the car keys.

They ran out again. Then they ran back inside to change out of their slippers.

'Where are my shoes?' Lady B shouted to Sir B as she searched through her empty shoe cupboards.

'I don't anything about that either,' he lied.

She pulled on a pair of old garden boots and ran for the front door. They were passing the living room when they heard a noise from inside. They stopped to peer in.

SuperBaby was seated on the carpet, eating ice cream out of a big tub. He had toys all around him and was offering them spoonfuls. There was a cat on the fish tank, fishing happily with one paw. A rat and a mouse were playing tug of war with a long piece of liquorice candy. A crow was watching a music video on the television and banging its head up and down in time to the music.

'Gooboo wongaponga!' the baby gurgled at the kidnappers. 'Gotcha!'

The babynappers turned and ran from the house.

The car drove off very fast, its tyres screeching. They didn't slow down until they were many miles away. Then Sir B glanced in the mirror.

'What's that on the back seat?' he whispered to Lady B.

'I hope it's not a baby,' she said. She turned to look. 'I… I think it's worse than that…'

Strapped into the middle seat was a green teddy coated in vegetable soup.

Christmas Four: Stealing the Sleigh

It's always good to give presents, even if it's your very first Christmas.

SuperBaby's parents were taking him to a big park as a celebration for escaping the kidnappers. They rode a bus there as a special adventure, talking happily about Christmas, which was tomorrow.

They stepped down from the bus and walked along the road to the park entrance… and stopped.

This part of the park was closed. There were tents inside the gates. People were sitting outside the tents, dressed in clothes that were different from the clothes that SuperBaby's family wore. There were some children running about, laughing and singing Christmas songs in a different language.

'I forgot they'd set up a refugee camp here,' said SuperBaby's father. 'We'll have to walk to the other side of the park.'

SuperBaby pointed at the children and his mother explained, 'Those are what we call *refugees*. They had to run away from their own country. Some of them are living in the park until we can find houses for them here. They don't have any money, you see.'

'I feel sorry for the children,' said his father. 'Their parents won't be able to afford any Christmas presents this year.'

SuperBaby's mother saw that SuperBaby was starting to cry and added quickly, 'That's all right, because *Santa* will bring them presents!'

SuperBaby cried even harder. He knew Santa wasn't going to do that! Then he had a wonderful idea. He stopped crying. He laughed instead.

After SuperBaby's parents had gone to bed, SuperBaby put on his warmest jacket, gloves and tiny boots. He eased the window open quietly.

Cat the Cat whispered drowsily from beneath his cot, 'Where are you going?'

'I'm off to help Santa!'

The cat yawned. 'It's not safe for a baby to be outside all alone,' she said.

'But I *must* go!'

'Why?'

SuperBaby explained his plan.

Half an hour later, a flying baby was biting through the brightly coloured tape stretched across the front of Sir and Lady B's garage. It warned:

POLICE CRIME SCENE! DO NOT ENTER!

The tape parted and he pulled open the heavy doors of the garage. Some animals scampered inside and climbed onto the wooden seat of the sleigh. A scruffy crow flapped in and perched at the front.

Rocky the Rat said to Mick, 'You can't sit up here wiv us, Mick: you're gonna pull the sleigh.'

'Squeak?'

'We'll paint your nose red so it lights the way,' Cat the Cat added.

'Squeak?!!' A worried Mick climbed down.

SuperBaby scooped up the mouse. 'They're only joking, Mick,' he promised, putting him on the seat next to the others.

'Everyone ready?' he asked.

'Yeah. But how're you gonna do this?' Rocky asked. 'It's not a very big sleigh, but it's too heavy to pull by hand. You gonna hitch it to a car?'

'I'm going to fly it myself!' said SuperBaby. 'I've been eating lots of chocolate spread and doing some baby exercises to make me strong!'

He crawled underneath the sleigh and lifted it slowly. It started tilting backwards, so he put it down again and found a better place to lift it... and flew out of the garage with it.

Many people were awake at two o'clock on Christmas morning. Some of them rubbed their eyes and stared at Santa's sleigh skimming over the rooftops. Some heard mewing and squeaking. A few of them heard a baby voice saying things like:

'Weren't we supposed to turn left at the river, Connie?... *(Caw! No! Straight on!)* … Don't let Mick chew on the map! … It's really cold out here… Did Cat the Cat finish counting the presents? … *Ooops! Nearly dropped the sleigh!* … Just kidding! Stop crying, Mick, that was just a joke…'

The sleigh landed quietly inside the park. Four animals worked their way through the tents, counting children. A small shape flew between the sleigh and the tents, carrying presents.

'Just one kid here.'

'I got two in dis tent.'

'Caw – none in this nest.'

'Squeak squeak squeak squeak!'

There were enough presents to go around, with one left over.

'That one must be for you,' said Rocky.

SuperBaby looked longingly at the beautifully wrapped present. 'No,' he said. 'We'll give it to the little girl in the house near to Grandma's – the one we made laugh when we were looking for the Pink

Knicker Thief.'

They flew the empty sleigh back to its garage and shut the doors. SuperBaby stretched the police tape back across the doors and tied it. Then he flew his friends home, delivering the final present on the way. A very tired baby climbed into his cot and fell into a deep and happy sleep next to his best friends.

Inside the refugee tents, children were dreaming of Christmas presents. SuperBaby dreamed about a flying sleigh guided by a cat, a rat, a mouse and a scruffy crow. Cat the Cat dreamed about a giant tin of Christmas sardines. Rocky dreamed about warm chips with salt and vinegar. Connie dreamed about a nest made from liquorice and cotton candy. Mick had a nightmare about an owl with big scary eyes that wanted to play a game of Scrabble with him.

When they woke, they all had a very happy Christmas.